THE ALIEN INTELLIGENCE

By
JACK WILLIAMSON

I0541518

ARMCHAIR FICTION
PO Box 4369, Medford, Oregon   97501-0168

AT THE EDGE OF AN UNKNOWN ABYSS

At the lip of a forgotten crater deep in the Mountain of the Moon, a silver ladder stretched downward through clouds of red and purple mist. Far below waited a crystal city, a beautiful woman, and alien horror…

On Earth, having an above-average need for adventure, Winfield Fowler did not for one second question his duty in responding to his dear friend's radioed pleas for help. Promptly, he gathered the items his friend had requested. He then provisioned three ponies for a grueling desert trek and set off into the barren sandy seas of Australia's wasteland. But what would he find there?

Master science fiction writer Jack Williamson gives us one man's harrowing account of his journey to the depths of an alien territory—found right here on Earth!

FOR A SECOND COMPLETE NOVEL, TURN TO PAGE 93

CAST OF CHARACTERS

WINFIELD FOWLER
With no hesitation, this man set out on an enterprise toward the unknown in order to help his friend…if he could only find him!

HORACE AUSTEN
Having vanished into the Great Victoria Desert weeks before, his insistent short wave transmissions for aid were most alarming.

MELVAR
As a maiden of the crystal city, she was expected to fear and distrust the newcomers. Yet she was not fearful, only curious…

NARO
Melvar's loyal, heroic brother. He bared the scars of past battles, but with his sister's life at stake, he was ready to fight again!

JORAK
He was the feared and reviled leader of the city of Astran. His wicked and despicable sacrifices marked every citizen.

THE KRIMLU
These monstrous creatures possessed mighty airships that emitted lightning quick red streaks of dread

THE PURPLE ONES
From the purple mist they came. Long white hair, sometimes bald, wrinkled and hideous, with red glaring eyes…

CHAPTER ONE
The Mountain of the Moon

BEFORE me, not half a mile away, rose the nearest ramparts of the Mountain of the Moon. It was after noon, and the red sun blazed down on the bare, undulating sandy waste with fearful intensity. The air was still and intolerably hot. Heat waves danced ceaselessly over the uneven sand. I felt the utter loneliness, the wild mystery, and the overwhelming power of the desert. The black cliffs rose cold and solid in the east—a barrier of dark menace. Pillars of black basalt, of dark hornblende, and of black obsidian rose in a precipitous wall of sharp and jagged peaks that curved back to meet the horizon. Needle-like spires rose a thousand feet, and nowhere was the escarpment less than half that high. It was with mingled awe and incipient fear that I first looked upon the Mountain of the Moon.

It was a year since I had left medical college in America to begin practice in Perth, Australia. There I had an uncle who was my sole surviving relative. My companion on the voyage had been Dr. Horace Austen, the well-known radiologist, archeologist, and explorer. He had been my dearest friend. That he was thirty years my senior, had never interfered with our comradeship. It was he who had paid most of my expenses in school. He had left me at Perth, and went on to investigate some curious ruined columns that a traveler had reported in the western part of the Great Victoria Desert. There Austen had simply vanished. He had left Kanowna, and the desert had swallowed him up. But it was his way, when working on a problem, to go into utter seclusion for months at a time.

My uncle was an ardent radio enthusiast, and it was over one of his experimental short wave sets that we picked up the remarkable message from my lost friend that led me to abandon my practice, and, heeding the call of adventure that has always been strong in those of my blood, to seek the half mythical Mountain of the Moon, in the heart of the unexplored region of the Great Victoria Desert of Western Australia.

The message was tantalizingly brief and hard to interpret. We picked it up five times, over a period of two weeks, always just after sunset. Evidently it was sent by one who had not recently practiced his knowledge of code, and it seemed that the sender was always in a great hurry, or under a considerable nervous tension, for minor errors and omissions were frequent. The words were invariably the same. I copy them from an old notebook.

"To Winfield Fowler, physician, Perth, Australia: I, Horace Austen, am lost in an unknown new world, where alien terrors reign that lies in a crater in the Mountain of the Moon. I implore you to come to my aid, for the sake of mankind. Bring arms, and my equipment, the Rontgen tubes and coils, and the spectrometer. Ascend ladder at west pinnacle. Find my friend Melvar, maiden of the crystal city, whom I left beyond the Silver Lake. Come, for the sake of civilization, and may whoever hears this forward it with all dispatch."

My uncle was inclined to suspect a hoax. But after the message had come over twice I received telegrams from several other radio amateurs who had heard it, and were forwarding it to me. We took the direction of the third call and had amateurs in Adelaide do the same. The lines intersected in the Great Victoria Desert, at a point very near that at which Wellington located the Mountain of the Moon, when he sighted it and named it in 1887.

Knowing Austen, as I did, to be intensely human as a man, but grave and serious as a scientist, it was impossible for me to take the message as a practical joke, as my uncle, deriding the possibility of my friend's being imprisoned in "an unknown new world," insisted it was. It was equally impossible for one of my impetuous and adventurous disposition to devote himself to any prosaic business when so attractive a mystery was beckoning him away. Then I would never, in any case, have hesitated to go to Austen's aid, if I knew him to be in need.

I got together the apparatus he had mentioned—it was some equipment he happened to have left with me as he went on—as well as my emergency medicine kit, a heavy rifle, two .45 Colt automatics, and a good supply of ammunition; and waited for more explicit signals. But the calls had never come regularly, and after the fifth no more were heard. Having waited another irksome week, I bade my uncle farewell and got on the train. I left the railway at Kanowna, and bought three ponies. I rode one and packed provisions, equipment, and water bottles on the other two. Nothing need be said of the perils of the journey. Three weeks later I came in sight of the mountain.

Wellington had christened it as he did because of an apparent similarity to the strange cliff-rimmed craters of the moon, and the appellation was an apt one. The crags rose almost perpendicularly from the sand to the jagged rim. To climb them was clearly out of the question. The rock was polished slick by wind-blown sands for many feet, but rough and sharp above. To my left, at the extreme west point of the great curve, was a dark needle spire that towered three hundred feet above its fellows. I knew that it must be Austen's "west pinnacle." What sort of ladder I was to ascend, I had little idea.

As the sun sank back of the rolling sea of sand, dark purple shadows rose about the barrier, and I was struck with deep forebodings of the evil mystery that lay beyond it. The gold of the desert changed to silver gray, and the gray faded swiftly, while the deep purple mantle swept up the peaks, displacing even the deep red crowns that lay like splashes of blood upon the summits. Still I felt, or fancied, a strange spirit of terror that lurked behind the mountain, even in the night.

Quickly I made camp. Just two of the ponies were left, and they were near death (I have passed over the hardships of my trip). I hobbled them on a little patch of grass and brush that grew where water had run from the cliff; pitched my little tent, and found brush to start a tiny fire. I ate supper, with but a scanty cup of water; then, oppressed by the vast mysterious peaks that loomed portentously in the east, shutting out the starlight, I went in the tent and sought my blanket. Then came the first of those terrible and inexplicable occurrences that led up to the great adventure.

CHAPTER TWO
The Abyss of the Terror-light

FIRST I heard a faint whispering sound, or rather a hiss, infinitely far away, and up, I thought, over the cliffs. Then the cloth of the tent was lighted by a faint red glow thrown on it from above. I shivered and the strange spell of the mountain and the desert fell heavier upon me. I wanted to go out and investigate; but unfamiliar terror held me powerless. I gripped my automatic and waited tensely. The scarlet radiance shone ever brighter through the cloth. The sound turned to a hissing, shrieking scream. It was deafening, and it plunged straight down. It seemed to pause, to hover overhead. The red glare was almost blinding. Abruptly the tent was blown down by a sudden tempest of wind. For perhaps a minute the terror hung about me. I lay there in a strange paralysis of fear, while a hurricane of wind tore at the canvas upon me. I heard upon the tempest, above that awful whistling, a wild mad laugh that rang against the cliff, weirdly appalling. It was utterly inhuman, not even the laugh of a madman. Just once it rang out, and afterwards I imagined it had been my fancy.

Then the light and the sound swept up and away. With belated courage I tore my way from under the cloth. The stars were like jewels in the westward sky, where the zodiacal light was still visible. The ominous blackness of the mountain blotted out the eastern stars; and the peaks were lighted by a vague and flickering radiance of scarlet, like the reflection of unpleasant fires beyond. Strange pulsing, exploring fingers of red seemed to thrust themselves up from behind the cliff. Somehow they gave me the feeling that an incredibly great, incredibly evil personality lurked beyond. The crimson light shone weirdly on the wild summits of the mountain, as if they were smeared with blood.

I threw more brush on the fire, and crouched over it, feeling uncomfortably alone and terrified. When the flames had flared up I looked about for the ponies, seeking companionship even in them. They were gone! At first I thought they had broken their hobbles and run off, but I could neither see nor hear them, and they had been in no condition to run far. I walked about a little, to look for them, and then went back to the fire. I sat there and watched the eerie, unwholesome glare that shone over the mountain. No longer did I doubt the existence of Austen's "world where alien terrors reign." I knew, even as I had felt when I first saw the mountain that strange life and power lurked beyond it.

PRESENTLY I stretched the tent again, and lay down, but I did not sleep.

At dawn I got up and went to look for the ponies. I climbed one of the low dunes and gazed over the gray infinity of sand, but not a sign of them rewarded my look. I tried to trail them. I found where they had been hobbled, and followed the tracks of each to a place where the hoofs had cut deep in the sandy turf. Beyond there was no trace. Then I was certain of what I had already known, the Thing had carried them away.

Then I found something stranger still—the prints of bare human feet, half erased by the wind that had blown while the terror had hung there. That unearthly laugh, and the footprints! Was there a land of madmen behind the mountain? And what was the thing that had come and gone in the night? Those were questions I could not answer, but daylight dulled my wondering fear.

The sun would not rise on my side of the mountain until nearly noon, and the cold dark shadow of the cliff was upon me when the desert all about was a shimmering white in the heat of the sun. Austen's call had mentioned a ladder. I set out to find it. Just north of the peak I came upon it, running straight up like a silver ribbon to the top of the cliff. It was not the clumsy affair of ropes that I expected. In fact, I at once abandoned any idea that Austen had made it at all. It was of an odd-looking white metal, and it seemed very old, although it was corroded but little. The rungs were short white bars, riveted to long straps, which were fastened on the rock by spikes of the same silvery metal. I have said that the mountain rises straight from the sand. And the ladder goes on into the ground. That suggests that the sand has piled in on the base of the mountain since the ladder was put there. At any rate, I am sure that it is incredibly old.

I went back to camp; packed together my guns, a little food, and Austen's equipment; and started up the ladder. Although it was no more than six hundred feet to the top, heavily laden as I was, I got very tired before I reached it. I stopped several times to rest. Once, looking down on the illimitable sea of rolling sand, with the tiny tent and the sharp shadow of the mountain the only definite features, I had a terrible attack of vertigo, and my fears of the night returned, until I almost wished I had never started up the ladder. But I knew that if I were suddenly back in Perth again I would be more eager than ever to set out upon the adventure.

At last I reached the top and crawled up in the mouth of a narrow canyon, with the black stone walls rising straight to the peaks on either side. Down the crevice was a smooth curving pathway, very much worn, it seemed, more by time than human feet. It was not yet noon. I waited a few minutes to rest; then walked up the path with a very keen curiosity as to where it led. It grew so deep that the sky overhead was but a dark blue ribbon in which I saw Venus gleaming whitely. It widened. I walked out on a broad stone platform. And below me lay—the abyss.

I stood on the brink of a great chasm whose bottom must have been miles, even, below sea level. The farther walls of the circular pit—they must have been forty miles away—were still black in the shadow of the morning. Clouds of red and purple mist hung in the infinities of space the chasm contained, and completely hid the farther half of the floor. Beneath me, so far away that it was as if I looked on another world, was a deep red shelf, a scarlet plain weird as the deserts of Mars. To what it owed its color I could not tell. In the midst of the red, rose a mountain whose summit was a strange crown of scintillating fire. It looked as though it were capped, not with snow, but with an immense heap of precious jewels, set on fire with the glory of the sun, and blazing with a splendorous shifting flame of prismatic light. And the crimson upland sloped down—to "the Silver Lake." It was a lake shaped like a crescent moon, the horns reaching to the mountains on the north and the south. In the hollow of the crescent beyond, low hills rose, impenetrable banks of purple mist lying back of them to the dark wall in the distance. The lake gleamed like quicksilver and light waves ran upon it, reflecting the sunlight in cold blue fire. It seemed that faint purple vapors were floating up from the surface. Set like a picture in the dark red landscape, with the black cliffs about, the argent lake was very white, and very bright.

CHAPTER THREE
Down the Silver Ladder

FOR a long, long time I gazed into the abyss, lost in the wonder and the mystery of it. Meanwhile the sun climbed over and lit the farther rim, which still was black or dully red, because of the dark colors of the volcanic rocks of which it is composed. The scene was so vast, so strange, so wildly beautiful and unearthly, that it seemed almost a dream, instead of an ominous reality. It was hard to realize that somewhere upon the red plain, or along the shores of the Silver Lake, or perhaps beneath the banks of mist beyond, Austen was—or had been—alone, and in distress. I wondered, too, from what part of this strange world had come the thing of the whistling sound and the red light, which had taken the ponies.

It was well after noon before I ate a little lunch and took thought of the matter of descent. I saw that a second ladder led down in a fine line of silver until it disappeared above the crimson upland, miles below. I climbed over the brink and started down. Descending was easier than climbing had been, but I had infinitely farther to go. The soles of my shoes were cut through, and my hands became red and blistered on the rungs. Sometimes, when I was too tired to go on, I slung myself to the ladder with a piece of rope from my pack, while I rested.

Steadily the black walls rose higher about me. The red plateau beneath, the mountain with its crown of flaming gems, and the strange white lake beyond, came nearer and nearer.

I was still half a mile above the scarlet plain when the shadow of the western wall was flung fast over the valley floor, and the light purple mists beyond the argent lake deepened their hue to a dark and ominous purple-red.

But the Silver Lake did not darken. It seemed luminous. It gleamed with a bright, metallic silvery luster, even when the shadow had fallen upon it. Whenever I rested, I searched keenly the whole visible floor of the abyss, but nowhere was any life or motion to be seen.

With a growing apprehension, I realized that I would not have time to reach the ground before dark. I had no desire to be sticking like a fly to the face of the cliff when the Thing that had made the red light was moving about. Disregarding my fatigue and pain, I clambered down as fast as I could force my wearied limbs to move. The process of motion had become almost automatic. Hands and feet moved regularly, rhythmically, without orders from the brain. But sometimes they fumbled or slipped. Then I had to grasp, frenzied, at the rungs to save my life.

Night fell like a black curtain rolled quickly over the top of the pit, but the half-moon of the Silver Lake still shone with its white metallic light. And strange, moving shapes of red appeared in the mist in the hollow of the crescent. The light that fell upon the rock was faint, but still enough to help, and still I hurried—forcing hands and feet to follow down and find the rungs. And fearfully I looked over my shoulder at the bank of mist.

Suddenly a long pale finger of red—a delicate rosy ray—shot high out of it. And up the vague pathway it sped, a long slender pencil of crimson light—a narrow, sharp-tipped scarlet shape—high into the night, and over and around in a long arching curve. Down it plunged, and back into the mist. Presently I heard its sound—that strange whistling sigh that rolled majestically and rose and fell, vast as the roar of an erupting volcano. Other things sprang out of the purple bank, slender searching needles of brilliant scarlet, sweeping over the valley and high into the starlit sky above.

Following paths that were smooth and arched, with incredible speed, they swept about like a swarm of strange insects, always with amazing ease, and always shooting back into the cloud, leaving faint purple tracks behind them. And the great rushing sounds rose and fell. Those lights were incredible entities, intelligent—and evil.

They flew, more often than anywhere else, over the crown of lights upon the hill—the gems still shone with a faint beautiful glow of mingled colors. Whenever one swept near the mountain, a pale blue ray shot toward it from the cap of jewels. And the red things fled from the ray. More and more the flying things of crimson were drawn to the mountain top, wheeling swiftly and ceaselessly, ever evading the feeble beams of blue. Their persistence was inhuman—and terrible. They were like insects wheeling about a light.

All the while I climbed down as fast as I could, driving my worn-out limbs beyond the limit of endurance, while I prayed that the things might not observe me. Then one passed within a half mile, with a deep awful whistling roar, flinging ahead its dusky red pathway, and hurtling along with a velocity that is inconceivable. I saw that it was a great red body, a cylinder with tapering ends, with a bright green light shining on the forward part. It did not pause, but swept on along its comet-like path, and down behind the Silver Lake. Behind it was left a vague purple phosphorescent track, like the path of a meteor that lasted several minutes.

After it was gone, I hurried on for a few minutes, breathing easier. Then another went by, so close that a hot wind laden with the purple mist of its track blew against my face.

I was gripped with deathly, unutterable terror.

I let myself down in the haste of desperation. Then the third one came. As it approached it paused in its path, and drifted slowly and deliberately toward me. The very cliff trembled with the roaring blast of its sound. The green light in the forward end stared at me like a terrible, evil eye.

Exactly how it happened I never knew. I suppose my foot slipped, or my bleeding hands failed to grasp a rung. I have a vague recollection of the nightmare sensation of falling headlong, of the air whistling briefly about my ears, of the dark earth looming up below. I think I fell on my back, and that my head struck a rock.

In the Red Scrub

THE next I knew it was day, and the sun was shining in my eyes. I struggled awkwardly and painfully to my feet. My whole body was bruised and sore, and the back of my head was caked with dried blood. My exhausted muscles had stiffened during the night, and to stand upon my cut and blistered feet was torturing. But I had something to be thankful for—that I had been within a few feet of the ground when I fell; and that the red thing had departed and left me lying there, perhaps thinking me dead.

I leaned against the base of the metal ladder and looked about; I had fallen into a thicket of low red bushes. All about grew low thick brush, covering the slightly rolling plain. The plants were scarcely knee-high, bearing narrow, feathered leaves of red. The delicate, fern-like sprays of crimson rippled in the breeze like waves on a sea of blood. The leaves had a peculiar bright and greasy appearance and a strange pungent odor. The shrubs bore innumerable tiny snow-white flowers that gleamed like stars against the deep red background.

I think that the red vegetation had evolved from a species of *cycad*. Undoubtedly the greater crater had been isolated from the outer world when the great tree-ferns were reigning throughout the earth. And, as I was presently to find, the order of evolution in the deep warm pit had been vastly different from that which had produced man as its highest form of life. Presently I was to meet far stranger and more amazing things than the red bush. I am inclined to believe that the extraordinary color may have been due to the quality of the atmosphere, perhaps to the high pressure, or to the purple vapors that ever rose from the region beyond the Silver Lake.

Nowhere did I see any living thing, nor did I hear any sound of life. In fact one of the strange things of the place was the complete absence of the lower forms of life, and even of the smaller insects. The silence hung oppressively. It grew intolerably monotonous—maddening.

Far away to the right and to the left the walls of the pit rose straight and black to the azure infinity that arched the top. To the left of me, five or six miles away, towered the gem-crowned hill, its summit a blaze of ever-changing polychromatic flame. Beyond it, all along the east, the red plateau fell away to the Silver Lake, which lay like a curved scimitar of polished steel, with the faint bank of purple mist shrouding the low red hills that rose inside the curve beyond. The sun was just above the eastern peaks, shining purple through the mist.

After a time I limped slowly down the nearest of the little valleys. As I went my roving eye caught the bright glitter of brass on the ground at my feet. Searching in the red shrubs, I picked up three fired cartridges for a .45 caliber automatic. I held them in my hand and gazed over the weird scene before me, lost in wonder. They were concrete proof that Austen had passed this way, had here fought off some danger. He must yet be somewhere in this strange crater. But where was I to find *"Melvar, maiden of the crystal city,"* and what was she to do for me?

Presently I went on. I wanted water to bathe my cuts and bruises. I was very thirsty as well as hungry. My pack was an irksome burden, but I did not discard it, and I carried the heavy rifle ready in my hand. I was still feeling very weak. After a painful half mile I came to a tiny pool in a thicket of the red scrub. I lay down and drank the cool clear water until I was half sick. I threw away the remnants of my shoes and bathed my feet.

A Curious Sight

SUDDENLY my attention was arrested by a crystal clashing sound. There was a marching rhythm in it, and the clatter of weapons. I crouched down in the shrubbery and peered fearfully about. I saw a line of men, queerly equipped soldiers, marching in single file over the nearest knoll. They seemed to be wearing a closely fitting chain mail of silvery metal, and they had helmets, breastplates and shields that threw off the sunlight in scintillant flashes of red, as if made of rubies. And their long swords flashed like diamonds.

Their crystal armor tinkled as they came, in time to their marching feet.

One, whom I took to be the leader, boomed out an order in a hearty, mellow voice. They passed straight by, within fifty yards of me. I saw that they were tall men, of magnificent physique, white-skinned, with blond hair and blue eyes. On they went, in the direction of the fire-topped mountain, until they passed out of sight in a slight declivity, and the music died away.

It is needless to say that I was excited as by nothing that I had seen before. A race of fair-haired men in an Australian valley. What a sensational discovery! I supposed that they had built the metal ladder and come down it into the valley, but from whence had they come? Or was the Mountain of the Moon itself the cradle of humanity, the Garden of Eden?

Then the crystal weapons of the soldiery suggested that they used some transparent crystalline substance in lieu of metal, and that the iridescent crown upon the mountain might be the city of the race. Was it Austen's "crystal city?" That would suggest a high civilization, but I saw no sign of the mechanical devices that are the outstanding features of our own civilized achievement. Certainly the soldiers had carried no modern weapons.

Then I thought of the footprints and the eerie laugh. I wondered what contact Austen had had with these people. Had they been friends or foes? I wondered if it had been the men of the crystal city who had paid me a visit outside the cliffs. If so, the red torpedo-shapes of the night must be aircraft, and they must have advanced the art of aerial navigation to a very high degree.

I determined, first of all, to do some spying, and find out as much as possible about the strange race before I revealed my presence. I was not in a very good trim for battle, and I had taken much pain for concealment when the men passed.

But I had little doubt that my guns were so far superior to their crystal swords that I could fight them at any odds if they proved unfriendly.

So presently I bound my feet with bandages from my medicine kit, attended as best I could to the wound on the back of my head, and walked slowly in the direction of the mountain, keeping in the cover of the valleys as much as possible. Although I could limp painfully along, the red vegetation offered me no very serious impediment to my progress. The low bushes crushed easily underfoot, burdening the air with their unfamiliar, pungent odor. The country was rolling, the low hills and level valleys all covered crimson with the scrub, gigantic boulders scattered here and there. The Silver Lake shimmered in the distance—a bright, white, metallic sheet.

The gem-capped mountain rose before me until I saw that the gaunt black sides rose a full thousand feet to the crown of blazing crystal. And as I drew nearer, I saw that indeed the gems were buildings, of a massive, fantastic architecture. A city of crystal! Prismatic fires of emerald-green, and ruby-red, and sapphire-blue, poured out in a mingled flood of iridescence from its slender spires and great towers, its central ruby dome and the circling battlements of a hundred flashing hues.

CHAPTER FOUR
Melvar of Astran

JUST before noon I staggered into a little dell that was covered with unusually profuse growths of the crimson plants. Along a little trickling stream of water they were waist high, bearing abundantly the star-shaped flowers, and small golden-brown fruits. Suddenly there was a rustling in the thicket and the head and shoulders of a young woman rose abruptly out of the red brush. In her hand she held a woven basket, half full of the fruits. In my alarm I had thrown up the rifle. But soon lowered it and grinned in confusion when I realized that it was a girl, and by far the most beautiful one I had ever seen. I have always been awkward in the presence of a beautiful woman, and for a few minutes I did nothing but stand and stare at her, while her quizzical dark, blue eyes inscrutably returned my look.

She was clad in a slight garment, green in color that seemed to be woven of a fine-spun metal. Her hair was long and golden, fastened behind her shapely head with a circlet—a thin band cut evidently from a single monster ruby. Her features were fine and delicate, and she had a surpassing grace of figure. That her slender arms were stained to the elbows with the red juice of the plants—she had been picking the golden fruits—did not detract from her beauty. I was struck—and I will admit it, conquered—by her face. For a little time she stood very erect, looking at me with an odd expression, and then she spoke, enunciating the words very carefully, in a rich golden voice.

The language was English!

She said, "Are you—an American?"

"At your service completely," I told her. "Winfield Fowler, of White Deer, Texas, and New York City, not to mention other points. But I own to some surprise at finding a knowledge of the idiom in a denizen of so remote a locality."

"I can understand," she smiled. "But I think you could talk—more simply. So you are Winfield, who came with Austen across the great—ocean from America?"

"You guessed it," I said, trying to keep my growing excitement in hand, while I marveled at her beauty. "Is mind reading common in these parts?"

"Doctor Austen—the American—told me about you, his friend. And he gave me two books. Tennyson's poems, and—'The Pathfinder.'"

"So you have seen Austen?" I cried in real astonishment. "Are you Melvar? Are you the 'maiden of the crystal city?'"

"I am Melvar," she told me. "And Austen stopped in *Astran* one *sutar*—that is thirty-six days."

"Where is he now?" I eagerly demanded.

"He was a strange man," the golden voice replied. "He did not fear the *Krimlu,* as do the men of *Astran.* He walked off toward the pass in the north that leads around—around the Silver Lake, he called it. He had been watching the *Krimlu* as they came at night, and doing strange things with some stuff he took from—the Silver Lake. While he was here, the hunters brought in one of the—" again she hesitated, at a loss for a word. "—The Purple Ones," she concluded. "He took that to examine it."

"What are the *Krimlu?*" I exclaimed. "What—or who—are the Purple Ones? What is the Silver Lake?"

"You are a man of many questions," she laughed. For a moment she hesitated, with her blue eyes resting on my face.

"The *Krimlu,* so say the old men of *Astran,* are the spirits of the dead who come back from the land beyond the Silver Lake to watch the living, and to carry off the evil for their food. So the priests taught us, and so I believed until Austen came and told me of the world that is beyond. He told the Elders of the outer world, but they put upon him the curse of the sun, and drove him away. And indeed it is well that he was ready to go so willingly beyond the Silver Lake, for Jorak would have offered him to the Purple Sun had he been in the city another night."

Suddenly she must have become conscious of the intensity of my unthinking gaze, for she abruptly dropped her eyes, and flushed a little.

"Go on," I urged her. "What about the Purple Ones and the Silver Lake? Your account is certainly entertaining, if somewhat more mystifying than illuminating. At this rate you will have me a raving maniac in an hour, but the process is not unpleasant. Proceed."

Fowler Grows Bold

SHE looked up at me, smiled, looked off to the side, then let her eyes return to mine with curious speculation in them. "What is the Silver Lake," she went on, "you know as well as I, though Austen tried to find its secret. The touch of its water is death—a death that is terrible. And the Purple Ones—you will see them soon enough. They are strange beings who come, no one knows whence, into the land of *Astran*. The priests tell us that they are 'The Avengers of the Purple Sun'—but did you come down the ladder as Austen did?"

"Most of the way in the same manner," I told her. "I finished the descent rather faster than he did, I imagine."

"Is there really," she asked, "a broad world beyond, with fields and forests that are green, and seas that are of clear blue water, and a sun that is not purple, but white? Such Austen told me, but the elders say that the ladder is the path to the Purple Sun, and beyond is nothing. Is it true that there is a great nation of the men of your race, a nation of men who know the art of fire that Austen showed us, and greater arts, who can travel in ships over water and through the air like the *Krimlu?*"

"Yes," I said, "the world is that, and more, but, in all of it, I have never seen a girl so beautiful as you."

It is not my habit to make such speeches to ladies, but I was feeling a bit light-headed on that morning, as a reaction from my terrible adventure, and I was rather intoxicated by her charm.

She smiled, evidently not displeased, and looked away again, apparently composing her expression with difficulty. There was a suspicious twinkle in her dark blue eyes.

"Tell me why you have come into this land," she asked abruptly.

"Austen sent for me to come to his aid." I replied.

"You and Austen are not like the men of *Astran*," she mused. "Not one of them ever went out to face the *Krimlu* or even the Purple Ones, of his own free will. You must be brave."

"Rather, ignorant," I said. "Since I have seen the '*Krimlu*,' as you call the flying lights, I am about ready to give up my courage of any kind."

Then, because my exhausted condition had robbed me of my ordinary sense of responsibility, I did such a thing as I had never dared before. The girl was standing close before me, matchlessly beautiful, infinitely desirable. Her eyes were bright, and the sunlight glistened in her golden hair. And— well, I admit that I did not try very hard to resist the temptation to kiss her. I felt her arm at my back, a sudden quick thrust of her lithe body. The next I knew I was lying on my back, and she was bending over me, with tears in her eyes.

"Oh," she cried. "I didn't know. Your head! It is bleeding. And your hands and feet! I didn't notice!"

So I was compelled to lay there while the beautiful stranger very tenderly dressed and bandaged the cut on my head. In truth, I doubt that I would have been able to get up immediately. The touch of her cool fingers was very light and deft. Once her golden hair brushed against my cheek. Her nearness was very pleasant. I knew that I loved her completely, though I had never taken much stock in love at first sight.

Presently she had finished. Then she said, "When Austen gave me the books he left a letter for any man of the outside who might happen to come to *Astran*. You must come with me to the city to get it, and to rest until you can walk without limping so painfully. Then, if you will, you can go on around the northern pass. Perhaps you can find Austen. But the *Krimlu* are mighty. No man of *Astran* has ever dared oppose them. No man who has ever gone into that accursed region has ever been seen again."

CHAPTER FIVE
Astran, the Crystal City

THE sun dropped beneath the rim, and the purple dusk began to thicken and to creep over the valley floor. I took up my precious equipment, and Melvar and I walked off through the red brush in the direction of the mountain. The vast, strange buildings of the city of gems were still glowing with soft color, and the cold, bright surface of the Silver Lake flashed often into sight beyond the rolling eminences. Presently we came to a well-worn path through the crimson scrub, but I saw nothing to indicate that anyone had thought of paving or improving it. But the *Astranians* did not seem to have much energy for any kind of public work. Their material civilization appeared to be on a rather low scale. In fact they supplied their wants in the way of food entirely with the abundant fruit of the red bushes. As I had guessed from the girl's remarks, they did not even have the use of fire. Indeed the great physical and mental development of the race and the splendid city in which it lived was strangely contrasted with their absolute lack of scientific knowledge.

Our pace was hastened by thoughts of the terrors that night would bring, and perhaps because of them, we walked nearer one another, and presently we were hurrying along, hand in hand. About us the purple night deepened and, beyond the argent brilliance of the Silver Sea, the strange evil of the night gathered itself for the attack.

At last we came to the narrow path that wound up the side of the mountain to the splendid palaces that crowned it. We hurried; came to a great arched gate in the emerald wall, and entered. The huge, incredibly magnificent buildings were scattered irregularly about the summit, with broad spaces between them. Here and there were paved courts of the silvery metal, which must have been an aluminum bronze, but the open ground was for the most part grown up in rank thickets of the red brush. The great building showed the wear and breakage of ages. Here and there were great heaps of gleaming crystal, where wonderful edifices had fallen, with the brush grown up around them. Incredible as it may seem, I think the old civilization of *Astran* had possessed a science that was able to synthesize diamonds and other precious stones, in quantities sufficient even for use as building stone. Later I had an opportunity to examine bits of the fallen masonry.

Towering above all, on the very peak of the mountain, was a great ruby dome, vast as the dome of St. Peter's, and mounted upon the center of the top was a huge machine that resembled nothing so much as a great naval gun, though it was made of crystal and white metal. A little group of men were gathered about it, and as I watched they swung the great tube about and a narrow ray of pale blue light poured out of it. And down on the plain below, where the practice beam had struck, a great boulder flashed into sudden incandescence. In their exploration of the ultraviolet spectrum, our own scientists have found rays that are strangely destructive to life, and considerable progress has been made in the development of a destructive beam of wireless energy. But later I was to meet a far more terrible ray weapon than that slender blue beam.

"With that," said Melvar, "our people fight off the *Krimlu* at night. But the *Krimlu* are so many that sometimes they are able to land and take our people. If only we had more of the beams. But there is no man in all *Astran* who knows how the light is made, or anything save that the blue light shines out to destroy when rock of a certain kind is put into the tube. Austen wished to examine it, and spoke of something he called 'radium ore' but the priests forbade. Indeed, his curiosity is one of the reasons Jorak had for driving him away."

Standing about the ill-kept streets were a few of the people of the crystal city. All were of magnificent physique, and intelligent looking, white-skinned, and fair haired. All wore garments that seemed of spun metal, and gleaming crystal weapons. Most of them were hurrying along, intent on affairs of their own, but a few gathered around us almost as soon as we stepped in the gate. I felt that they were hostile to me. They questioned Melvar in a tongue that was strange to my ears; then became engaged in a noisy debate among themselves. Their glances toward me were furtive and sullen, and their eyes had the look of men crazed by fear.

Safe!

MELVAR was saying something in a conciliatory tone, and I was swinging my rifle into position for use, when there was a sudden shout from the gate of the city, and the clashing of crystal weapons. The interruption was most welcome to me. The crowd turned eagerly to the new arrivals. I saw that they were a band of soldiers, possibly the same that had passed me in the morning. Slung to a pole carried between the foremost two, was a strange thing. Weirdly colored and fearfully mutilated as it was, I saw that it was the naked body of a human being. The head was cut half off, and dangling at a grotesque angle. The hair was very long and very white, flying in loose disorder. The features were withered and wrinkled, indeed the whole form was incredibly emaciated. It was the corpse of a woman. The flesh was deep purple!

As I stood staring at the thing in horror, there was laughter and cheering in the crowd, and a little child ran up to stab at the thing with a miniature diamond sword. Melvar touched my arm.

"Come," she whispered. "Quickly. The people do not like your coming. They did not like the things Austen told of the world outside, for the priests teach that there is no such world. It is well that the hunters came when they did with the Purple One. And let us hope that the priests of the Purple Sun do not hear of you."

As she spoke she led me rapidly away through a tangle of the red brush, and through a colonnade of polished sapphire. Then she quickly led the way down a deserted alley, across another patch of the red shrubbery, and down a short flight of steps into a chamber that was dark.

"Wait here," she commanded. "I must leave you. I think that Jorak has had spies upon me, and if I were too long absent he might grow suspicious. He was the enemy of my father, and some day my brother will slay him. But sometimes I am afraid of the way he looks at me. However there is no danger now. If the priests hear, I will somehow get you out of *Astran*. I think they will not seek you here, whatever may happen. My brother will bring the message from Austen, and food and drink. May you rest well, and have faith in me."

She ran up the steps, and left me standing in the darkness, in a state of uncomfortable indecision. I did not like the turn that affairs had taken. It is never pleasant to be alone in the dark in a strange and dangerous place. I would have much preferred to take my chances out on the open plain, with nothing but the moving lights to fear, terrible as they were, than here in this strange city, full of ill-disposed savages. A diamond knife will kill a man just as effectively and completely as the weirdest death that ever roamed the night.

For a time I stood waiting tensely, with my rifle in my hand, but I was very tired and weak. Presently I got out my flashlight and examined the place. It was a little cell, apparently hewn in the living rock of the mountain. There was nothing in the way of furniture except a sort of padded shelf, or bed; at the back. I sat down upon it, and presently went to sleep there, though I had no intention of doing so.

Austen's Letter

THE next I knew, someone was shaking my arm, and shouting strange words in my ear. I opened my eyes. Standing before me was a young man. In one hand he held a crystal globe filled with a glowing, phosphorescent stuff, faintly lighting the little apartment. I sat up slowly, for my limbs were stiff. The gun was still in my hand. Without saying anything more, the young fellow pointed to a tray that he had set by me on the shelf. It contained a crystal pitcher of aromatic liquid, and a dash of the yellow fruit. I gulped down some of the drink, and ate a few of the fruits, feeling refreshed almost immediately. Then the boy—he was not more than sixteen years of age—thrust into my hand an envelope addressed in the familiar handwriting of Austen. He handed me the light and walked up the stone stairs.

With feeling that well may be imagined, I tore open the envelope and read, in the faint light of the glowing bulb, the words of my old friend.

> "*Astran*, in the Mountain of the Moon.
> June 16, 1927.

"To whomsoever of my own race this may be delivered:

"Since you must so far have traveled the mysterious dangers of this strange world, it is needless for me to dwell upon them. I write this brief missive for the information of anyone who shall happen to find the way in here in the future, and in order that the riddle of my own disappearance may some time be cleared up, if I fail to return. For I intend to explore the region beyond this lake—I call it the Silver Lake—or to lose my life in the attempt.

"My name is Horace Austen. I came to the Great Victoria Desert to investigate the sculptured columns reported by Hamilton, far to the west of here. I found the ruins and incredibly ancient they are. They must date from fifty thousand years ago, at the latest. Among them was an amazing pictographical record of a race of men driven by the drying up of their country to emigrate to the crater of a great mountain nearby. There was no mistaking the meaning. I was, of course, intensely interested, for nothing of the kind had ever been reported in Australia, and certainly the people depicted were not Bushmen.

"It happened that I remembered Wellington's account of the Mountain of the Moon, whose northern cliff was followed for a few miles by his route of 1887. That appeared to be the best chance for the great crater described on the columns. It was but natural for me to decide to investigate it. There is no use for me to dwell upon my hardships, but the last of my water was drunk when I found the ladder, which was located just as the inscriptions indicated.

"I reached the red plain without accident, and found the fruit of the strange vegetation a palatable and nourishing food. So far I have escaped the red lights that haunt the night, and it is their mystery that I am determined to solve. I went down to the metallic lake, and investigated it. I confess myself quite unable to account either for the nature or for the incredible origin of the fluid. With proper precaution it can be studied without great difficulty, but since I am almost entirely without apparatus, I have learned little enough about it.

"I had been in the crater a week when I decided to approach the city of jewels on the mountain. I have been in *Astran* over a month, but on account of the savagery and ignorance of the people, and the oppressive rule of the priesthood, I have not been on very friendly relations with them—with the exception of the girl, Melvar, who seems far above the others of her race, and who has been my friend from the first. I have been able to learn but little from them, although I have acquired a fair knowledge of the language. My instructor in it, the beautiful Melvar, is showing a keen desire to learn English, of which she is gaining a command with remarkable speed, and is developing, as well, an insatiable curiosity about the outer world.

"The sentiment against me has been ever running higher, and tomorrow I shall leave the crystal city, and endeavor to round the sea in the north and to reach the mist-veiled land beyond. My only regret in leaving is that I shall see Melvar no more. I wish there were some way to secure her the advantages of a civilized education.

"These may be my last words to the world, if indeed, they ever come into the hands of a civilized man. And I know that sooner or later the crater will be discovered and entered.

My chief purpose in writing this, aside from the satisfaction of leaving an account of my own doings is to state my firm belief, I may say, my certain knowledge, that the strange things that may be observed here, supernatural or incredible as they may appear, result from perfectly natural forces in the control of a civilized power that may not be much above our own advancements.

Horace Austen"

CHAPTER SIX
Fowler Recovers

I READ it in the faint glow of the phosphorescent globe, and read it again. So Austen was beyond the crescent, if he had been able to carry out his plan. The date of the letter was ten months back. Then the radio message had probably come from the other side. And why had it been sent? Austen was not one to appeal for aid for himself alone. Had he feared some general danger to the human race? I thought of his phrase, "for the sake of mankind," and shuddered at a picture of the red lights sweeping like destroying angels over a great city like New York decimating the terrorized population.

I tried to think what was best for me to do, if ever I got out of *Astran* alive. I supposed that Austen had been able to round the Silver Lake in the north. I should be able to follow him. Clearly there was nothing for me to do but to find out as much about this strange world as possible, and to get the equipment to him as soon as I could do so.

I stayed in the cellar-like home for a week. Twice each day the young chap came to bring food and drink. He knew but a few words of English, and during the hour or so he stayed each time I had him to try teaching me the language of *Astran*. But my progress was slow, and I never learned more than a few score words. The language seemed much more complex, even, than English, with bewildering rules of inflection. But I developed quite a liking for the boy. He had a simple, straight forward manner, and a good sense of humor. His name was Naro. He was the brother of Melvar, and two years younger. Their father, it seemed, had been carried off several years before, when the flying lights made a great raid, and the mother had soon after fallen a victim to the sacrificial rites of the hated Jorak. And the boy himself bore the scars of wounds he had suffered a few months before in a terrific battle with one of the Purple Ones, as those monsters were called, which so mystified me then, and with which I had such terrible experiences later.

On the second day Melvar came. She brought a great flask of aromatic oil that she poured over my wounds. It must have been remarkably healing, for in a few days I found myself entirely recovered. Before she left she told me that the priests had heard of my arrival, and that it was whispered among the people that I was a supernatural being, sent as an omen of an attack by the *Krimlu*. She told me, too, that there was talk that a sacrifice would soon be offered at the altar of the Purple Sun, to appease the angry Spirits of the dead. Sweet and innocent child, she seemed to have no fear that she, who had brought me into the city, would be the sacrifice, and I did nothing to let her know my misgivings, although I did propose that we leave the city together as soon as possible. How I hated to see her leave the apartment!

The Shrine of the Purple Sun

DURING the following days I questioned Naro constantly as to the doings of his sister, and of the *Astranians*, but I was able to elicit no very satisfactory information, except that none of the *Krimlu* had been seen for several days, and that the headmen of the nation were beginning to expect a raid in force. Also I persuaded him to keep a very close watch on the movements of Melvar, and to come to me at once if Jorak made any attempt to get her into his power, or if the sacrificial ceremony was begun with the victim unselected.

During the interminable periods when I was alone, I was driven almost insane by the monotony and the anxiety of my existence. But I had my scientific equipment, and I had the boy to bring me a few assorted fragments of the crystal building stone, which I tested and found to be real gems, of several varieties. Many of the gems were simple enough in chemical formula, and composed of the most common elements, so the synthesis of them by scientific means is not unreasonable.

For example, it is a well-known fact that diamond is just a crystal form of carbon, which element occurs in three allotropic forms. Those three forms are diamond, graphite, which also crystallizes, and amorphous carbon, of which charcoal is a form. Since carbon occurs in the air in carbon dioxide, it is not impossible that latter-day science would be able to manufacture diamonds from the air. Sapphires are aluminum oxide, or alumina, colored with a little cobalt, and rubies are composed of the same oxide, with a trace of chromium, to which the color is due. A clay-bed would supply an inexhaustible amount of the elements needed for the synthesis of these gems, and I think the people of old *Astran* had been able to accomplish it. I examined the little glow-lamp, too, and found it to be simply a crystal bottle filled with the moist crushed leaves of the red plants, which formed a culture of some kind of luminous bacteria.

On the seventh night, when the pale ray of daylight that filtered down into my hiding place was dim red, Naro burst into the chamber, panting, and wild-eyed with terror. His crystal sword was gone, his metallic mantle was torn, and blood was falling, drop by drop, from a deep scratch on his arm. He thrust into my hand a tattered scrap of paper, evidently the flyleaf of a book. On it, in an ink that I took at first to be blood, although it was probably the juice of the red plants, the following words were formed in hastily drawn printing characters:

"Winfield, there is no hope. The priests will offer a gift to the Purple Sun. I am the victim. Already I am in the hands of Jorak. I am sorry, for I loved you. It may be that I can give this to Naro, who could take it to you. The *Krimlu* are coming tonight. Already their lights flicker above the mist. In the morning my brother will take you to the gate, and you may escape. If only it had been one night later we might have all been away together. Farewell.

Melvar"

No time was to be lost. I had been anticipating something of the kind. The guns were cleaned and loaded. My pack was soon ready. Naro took a part of my equipment. I followed the boy up the stair, with the phrase, "For I loved you," ringing in my heart.

We reached the top and walked out into the red brush. Beneath the purple starlight the vast fantastic columned halls of *Astran* were gleaming faintly, and I caught a brief blue flicker from the great machine on the ruby dome.

Suddenly, with a sharp thrill of terror that made me catch my breath, I heard the awful distant whining sigh that grew until it rolled and reverberated through the heavens, and the air seemed alive with its deep intensity. Above the emerald wall I glimpsed the green-tipped needle of crimson that made the sound. It was sweeping through the sky meteor-swift, while the pale blue beam stabbed out at it ineffectually. It passed in an instant, but others came, and soon the sky was lighted with the weird red radiance, and the very mountain top vibrated with the whistling roars. The things swept around and around in a mad confusion of darting flames. They were like moths about a candle.

We passed an amber palace wall and came suddenly upon a great, metal-floored court. Marching across it were a half score of the *Astranian* men-at-arms, their accoutrements gleaming weirdly in the light of the strange things above. They saw us at once, and charged upon us with a shout. I dropped to my knees. Once my rifle spoke, and I rejoiced at its heavy thrust against my shoulder, and the acrid odor of the smoke. I felt a man again. And the leader of the soldiers fell upon his face.

Melvar Saved

NARO gripped my shoulder and pointed upward. One of the red things was plunging down, like a great red Zeppelin with a great green light at its forward end, its purple phosphorescent track swirling up behind it. The soldiers forgot us and scattered in mad terror. Naro jerked my arm and in a moment we had tumbled into a copse of the red brush. For a moment the bloody radiance was thrown upon us in an intense flood, and the screaming roar was deafening. A few minutes more, and the thing had flashed up and away. A breath of hot purple mist passed over us. When we got to our feet and crept out of the thicket the soldiers were gone.

Swiftly, Naro led me on, keeping in the shadows of the building, or in the cover of the thickets. Once a man sprang suddenly at us from behind a sapphire pillar, diamond sword drawn. My pistol exploded in his face and blew his head half off. Naro possessed himself of the dead man's weapons, and we went breathlessly on. Three times, in other parts of the city, we saw the red shapes drop to the ground for a few minutes, and then dart up again, while ever the blue ray played back and forth upon them.

At last we passed between vast ruby columns and stood beneath the huge red dome. Before us lay a great space, fairly lit with a rosy light from the crystal walls. Around the farther side were seated tier upon tier, thousands of the brilliantly clad people of *Astran*. In the center of the great floor, resting upon a pedestal, was a globe of shining purple—a sphere of coruscating flame—itself immense, perhaps forty feet in diameter, but insignificant in that colossal hall. Standing at rigid attention, in regular rows about the pedestal were a few score bright-armed soldiers, and as many other erect men in long purple robes. All eyes were fixed on a point in front of the gigantic globe, and hence hidden from where we stood.

We hurried silently across the smooth metal floor, our footsteps drowned in the rushing sounds of the flying things above. We ran around the great purple sun-sphere of crystal, and came abruptly upon a dramatically terrible scene. Beneath the sphere was an altar of glowing red, with the priests and soldiery all grouped about it. By the altar, kneeling and silent, clad in a filmy green robe, was the beautiful form of Melvar. Just behind her stood a tall hawk-like man, in his hands a great transparent crystal vessel full of a liquid that gleamed like molten silver.

As we came around the sphere he was holding up the vessel and repeating a strange chant in a monotonous monotone. At sight of us he dropped into alarmed silence, with an ugly scowl of hate and fear distorting his harsh features. For a moment he stood as if paralyzed, then he rushed toward the silent girl as though to empty the contents of the crystal pitcher upon her.

I fired on the instant, and had the luck to shatter the vessel, splashing the shining silvery fluid all over his person. The effect of it was instantaneous and terrible. His purple robe was eaten away and set on fire by the stuff; his flesh was dyed a deep purple, and partially consumed. He tottered and fell to the floor in a writhing, flaming heap.

In the confusion, and the dazed silence that fell upon the vast assemblage at sight of that horrible thing, Melvar, aroused from her resignation of despair by the report of the pistol, sprang to her feet in incredulous surprise. For a moment she looked wonderingly at us. Then she turned and shouted a few strange and impressive words at the priests. Her white arms swept up in a curious gesture.

Then she turned and sped toward us. We started running back the way we had come. The dramatic fall of Jorak, and the evident terror that Melvar's courageous and timely words, whatever they had been, had inspired, served to hold the *Astranians* motionless until we had traversed the better part of the distance to the columns. But then they started after us en masse. I dropped to my knees at the columns and began firing steadily with the rifle. They fell, sometimes two or three at a shot, but still they charged on, and their number was overwhelming.

Then, outside, there was a sudden louder shrieking roar. A flood of red light poured through the columns, and there was a terrific crash upon the dome. Dense clouds of hot purple vapor poured into the vast room. One of the flying lights had landed upon the roof. The charging throng behind us stopped and ran about in confusion. We darted out through the purple clouds and ran for the shadow of the nearest building. We kept close by the mighty walls until we reached the gate. Daring the terrors of the night, we ran out and down the narrow trail. By dawn we were several miles from *Astran* in the direction of the shining lake.

CHAPTER SEVEN
The Silver Lake

AT the coming of day we were walking over a gently rolling scarlet plain, scattered with gigantic solitary boulders that sloped gradually down to the Silver Lake. The lake lay flat and argent white, clad in all the ominous mystery of that strange world, calling, beckoning us on, challenging us to learn the secret of the farthest bank of purple fog, with a grim warning of the doom that might await us. The red fern-like sprays waved gently in the breeze, and the vivid, tiny white flowers seemed to sparkle with a million glancing rays, like frost in the sunshine; but the deep intensity of the red color lent a weird and unpleasant suggestion of blood. Beyond the Silver Lake, low hills rose, faint and mysterious in the purple haze.

Melvar walked beside me when the way was smooth enough; she was talking vivaciously. She had a keen sense of humor and a lively wit. She seemed to have an almost childishly perfect faith in my power and that of my guns— but I was far from feeling confident.

At sunrise we stopped by a little pool of clear water, drank, and made a meal of the abundant yellow fruit. *Astran*, with the scintillating fires kindled again in its jeweled towers by the rising sun, lay far behind and above us. When we had finished eating, Melvar stood looking for a long moment at its glorious sparkling light. She murmured a few words beneath her breath, in the *Astranian* tongue, and turned again toward the Silver Lake.

In two hours we came to the shore of the great lake. The red scrub grew up to the brink of a bluff a dozen feet high. Below was a broad, bare sandy beach, with the gleaming waves, quicksilver white, rolling on it two hundred yards away. For a few minutes we stood at the edge of the cliff in the fringe of crimson brush, and let our eyes wander over the vast flat desert of flowing argent fire. We peered at the misty red hills beyond, trying to penetrate their mysteries, and to read what lay behind them. Then we scrambled down on the hard white sand. Naro grasped his weapon and looked up and down the beach.

"It is along the shore of the Silver Lake," Melvar said, "that the Purple Ones are most frequently found."

"The Purple Ones, again!" I cried. "What are they— decorated rattlesnakes?" Then, with a sickening sensation of terror, I remembered the horrible, half-human purple corpse that I had seen the soldiers bringing into *Astran*. "Are the Purple Ones men?"

"In form, they are men and women," Melvar said, "but they dwell alone in the thickets like beasts. All of them are old and hideous. They are savage, and they have the strength each of many men. Our soldiers must always hunt them, and fight them to the death. A single man, even though armed, could do nothing against one of them, for they are terribly strong, and they fight like demons. Their country is not known, and no children of their kind are ever found. The priests say that they are of a race of dwarfs that dwell beneath the Silver Lake."

Here was another of the baffling mysteries of this strange world. In fact, I was coming upon unpleasant mysteries much faster than I could comfortably stomach them. Lone, purple, savage animals, in the form of emaciated humans, who prowled about the country like wolves, and like wolves were hunted down by the *Astranians!* Again I shuddered at the memory of the limp purple corpse the soldiers had carried, and with a strange chill of the heart, I remembered the human footprints that had been left where my ponies were taken in the desert, and of the eerie, insane laughter that I had heard, or thought I heard, above the whistling roar.

My thoughts ended with the construction of a mad hypothesis of a race of purple folk who lived beyond the Silver Lake, who were accustomed to make slave raids on the whites in torpedo-shaped airships, and who made a practice of releasing, or turning out, the superannuated ones of their kind to prey on the people of the crystal city. It seemed, in fact, quite plausible at the time, but I was far from the hideous truth. I could see no reason, if one race could attain a civilization high enough to synthesize diamonds for building stone, why another might not be able to build ships as marvelous as the red torpedoes. But my reason rebelled at the acceptance of the ideas of demonic and supernatural horrors my emotional self tried to force upon it.

The Touch of the Metal

PRESENTLY I roused myself and led the way down to the white waves. My companions held back nervously and warned me not to touch it, or I would die as Jorak had done. But I succeeded in filling a test tube with the stuff. It was not transparent. It was white, gleaming, metallic, like mercury, or molten silver. I carried it back up to the bluff and set about examining it, while Naro stood guard, and Melvar watched me. She asked innumerable questions, concerning not only the operation in hand, but on such subjects as the appearance of a cat, and Fifth Avenue styles of ladies' garments. Upon which (the latter subject), however, I was lamentably ignorant. And so often did I pause, to answer her questions, to laugh at the naive quaintness of her phrases, or to let my eyes rest on her charming face, that the attempted analysis of the metal did not progress with any remarkable celerity.

The silver liquid was very mobile and very light, having a specific gravity of only .25, or not even four times that of liquid hydrogen, which is .07. It was extremely corrosive.

Tiny bits of wood or paper were entirely consumed on contact with it, with the liberation, apparently, of carbon dioxide and water vapor, and a dense purple gas that I could not identify. That suggested, of course, that the stuff contained oxygen, but as to how much, or in what combination, I had no idea. A drop of it on a larger piece of paper set it afire. I found, too, when testing the electrolytic qualities of the liquid, that when I introduced into it a copper and a silver coin, electrically connected, that the stuff was rapidly decomposed into the purple vapor, with the generation of a powerful current. But the metal seemed not affected at all. That was another puzzling result. My experiments, of course, were comparatively crude, and when I had gone as far as I could, I really knew little more about the silver liquid than in the beginning.

Despite Melvar's warning, and my own precautions, I splashed a drop of it on my arm. She cried out in horror, and I saw that a splotch of purple was spreading like a thin film over the skin. There was no pain, but the muscles of the arm were seized with sudden and uncontrollable convulsions. Melvar tried to wash the stain off with water from my canteen. In an hour the color had faded, though the limb was still sore and painful.

By that time, the purple disc of the sun was sinking low, and we took thought of how to spend the night. Naro climbed up on the plain to gather a few of the fruits for our supper, and we found a little cave in the bluff that seemed a good place of shelter. I gathered an armful of the red brush and made a fire.

The leaves burned fiercely, crackling as if they contained oil. The fire produced a great volume of acrid black smoke. Combustion was greatly accelerated on account of the increased atmospheric pressure here, many thousand feet below sea level. Melvar and Naro were intensely interested in the performance, although they had seen Austen light a fire while he was in the city.

Melvar slept in the cavern, and Naro and I took turns at standing guard at the entrance. The darting pencils of crimson were abroad again, but they passed far overhead, and we heard the sounds of their passage only as vast and distant sighs. In the morning we rose early, and clambered back up the cliffs. I was in rather a puzzling situation. Clearly my duty was to get Austen's equipment to him as quickly as possible, but I liked neither to desert Melvar and her brother, nor to let them accompany me into the unknown perils of the region beyond. But the latter course seemed the best, and they were ready enough to go with me anywhere.

The Land of Madness

HAVING retraced our course of the day before for perhaps a mile, in order to get upon the upland, we set out for the north. The sun was just rising above the black rim when Naro shouted and pointed at the mist-clad red hills beyond the Silver Lake. At first I looked in vain; then I caught a faint flicker of amber light, pulsing up through the purple air.

Abruptly a vast mellow golden beam of light sprang from behind the distant scarlet hills and spread up toward the zenith in a deep yellow flood. It seemed to vibrate, to throb with incredibly rapid fluctuations. Suddenly, bright swift-changing formless shapes of green and red flared up within it, shot up the beam, and vanished. The radiance dimmed and died. I could see nothing, but somehow I felt that an invisible beam of vibrant force was still pouring up into the sky. Here was another manifestation of the unknown power beyond the sea. The beam had come. So far as visibility was concerned, it was gone. What had been its meaning, its purpose?

Beyond the Silver Lake, low cliffs rose above a broad sandy beach, faintly veiled by the purple mist. The red hills were fainter still above them, and the thicker pall of purple haze that hung over the hidden place beyond, stood out distinctly against the distant, steep black wall that threw his jagged crags to the sky so far above. Out of that vale of mystery the ray had leapt—and died. Or had it merely faded, and was now, invisible…pulsing still?

All seemed as it had been before, but from the attitude of my companions I knew there was more to come. They were gazing up into the sun-bright void above and waiting expectantly.

Then I saw, far, far above, growing gradually brighter against the sky, as if it were being projected there by a great magic lantern behind the hills, an upright bar of silver haze. Slowly it grew brighter and its outlines sharper until it looked like a vertical bar of silver metal in the sky—inconceivably huge. The length of the bar must have been miles, its diameter, many hundreds of yards. It hung still in the heavens, neither rising nor falling. Here was the display, indeed, of alien science and power.

Presently I recovered from my first wonder, and became conscious that the blue eyes of Melvar were upon me quite as much as on the astonishing thing in the sky. "Melvar, have you seen it before?" I asked. "Is it real—natural? Is it made by man?" I found to my surprise that my voice was odd and quavery. I had not realized the intensity of my nervous strain. I waited eagerly for the reassurance that she could not give.

"It comes often," she replied. "Every day for many months of the year. The priests say that it is the evil goddess of the under-earth, who loves the Purple Sun and flies to the sky to meet him. But the Sun goes on unheeding, and the goddess cries silver tears until her Lord is gone from the sky. But there is yet more to see."

I looked up again and saw that a faint colored mist was gathering about the bar. It grew brighter, condensed, seemed drawn into swirling rings by a sort of magnetic attraction. And the iridescent mist-rings swam about the bar, moved ever faster until they were whirling madly. Their coruscating shapes grew brighter, plainer, until they were vivid, spinning flames of color in the sunshine. I noticed that the red was about the center of the silver bar, and that the bands of color above and below ran regularly to the other end of the spectrum, with rings of violet at the bottom and at the top. During all this time I heard no sound. It was as still as death.

Still the color-rings spun and changed, growing ever brighter and sharper edged. The red band grew larger about the center, until its diameter was the length of the cylinder. It gleamed with a lurid scarlet light. Below and above were spinning, burning circles of orange, yellow, green, and blue, each thinner than the one next nearer the center, and of smaller diameter. And the violet rings had shrunk to great globes of violet fire, shining with painful intensity.

Indeed, as Melvar had said, there had been more to see. The thing was so utterly strange, so utterly inexplicable, that I was grasped in a paralysis of unfamiliar terror, my breath choked off and my heart beating wild with fear, staring straight at it. It was so definitely directed by intelligence that I felt it must spring from a weird and awful mind. Indeed, it seemed that I felt the power of a vast and alien will stealing over me, seizing command of me, making me the slave of itself. I struggled against it. I clenched my hands and knotted my muscles with the intensity of my resistance to the spell. Wheeling sparks of red fire swam before my eyes.

Then my efforts weakened. I could hold out no longer. The alien will had won. Reason and feeling and love flowed away and left me as cold and cruel as a rock in a stormy, wintry coast—a savage, inhuman animal. Care had left me. My soul had lost her throne. I laughed. A wild, unearthly sound it was, like that I had heard as I lay beneath the tent beyond the barrier.

I whirled around fiercely, but a firm arresting hand was laid on my shoulder. From afar off, deep blue eyes looked into mine—eyes that were cool and sane and brave. They shone through the red curtains of insanity in my brain. They broke the spell of fear.

Suddenly I was very weak, and trembling and sick. Melvar's lithe arms were close about me. Her throbbing heart was close to mine. And in her dark, warm blue eyes, so close to mine, were sympathy, and tenderness, and love. She was human; she was real. I knew that her love would shield me from these terrors. I smiled at her, and sank down weakly in the red brush. But she had saved my mind. I had wandered on the brink of the fearful insanity of terror, and she had brought me back.

I looked from her sweet face, so full of anxious concern to the thing in the sky. But now it seemed remote, unreal, and I gazed at it with weak indifference. Presently I saw that the whole thing was beginning to sink as though a weight were being accumulated upon it. Suddenly an immense gleaming globule of silver fell from the lower violet globe and dropped straight for the Silver Lake, while the weird form of lights that had made it floated back to its former elevation. The great shining sphere fell and struck the white lake with a deafening roar, sending out great concentric waves in all directions. The amazing thing sank again, released a second huge drop, and rose. The process was repeated again and again, the interval being, by my watch, about 3 minutes, 15.2 seconds. All day it went on, with the great waves washing up the bluffs above the beach, and before night the level of the Silver Lake stood perceptibly higher.

Here was the mystery of the origin of the Silver Lake explained, but by a phenomenon far more inexplicable than the sea itself. In vain I tried to account for it in some rational way, or to assign some natural cause for the thing. My mind could hardly grasp it. It was almost unbelievable, even as I looked upon it. My reason would not admit that such a thing could be in a rational world.

CHAPTER EIGHT
Stalked by the Purple Beast

SO weak was I after that terrible experience that it was noon before I felt able to go on. The thing, as I have said, continued to hang in the sky all day, and to drop regularly its burden of the silver liquid. But presently I became accustomed to it, and realized that it threatened us with no immediate danger.

After a light lunch of the yellow fruit, and a deep draught of water from a little stream that seemed almost parallel to our route of march for a mile or two, we retired to the higher ground where the scrub was not so dense as in the bottom of the valley, and set out for the north again. Still I was feeling mentally limp—duly indifferent to what was passing about— and physically exhausted as well. I was not as much on my guard against the weird perils of the place as I should have been.

Several times Naro stopped and listened, declaring that something was following us, keeping in the cover of waist-high brush in the bottom of the little valley along the side of which we were traveling. But I could hear nothing. Melvar, for once, had ceased her eager interrogation, and was entertaining me with the legendary account of the past great heroes of *Astran*. She sang me a few passages from the epic in her native tongue. Her voice was clear and pure and very beautiful. And though the words were strange to me, their sound was noble and suggestive, and there was a powerful, compelling rhythm in the lines. She translated the story into English. It was about such an epic poem as might have been expected, dealing with the adventures of an immortal hero; who had once conquered the Purple Ones, set up the vast palaces of *Astran*, and at last lost his life on an expedition across the Silver Lake to battle the *Krimlu*.

Suddenly her sweet voice was interrupted by a low, tense cry from Naro, who had fiercely gripped my arm. I turned in time to see a weird figure, gnarled and stooped, with long white hair, slink swiftly and furtively from a great rock to the shelter of the red brush. Squat and bent as it was, there was no mistaking that it was human in shape, and that the skin was purple.

In the dull apathy in which I was sunken, I could not realize the danger. "I guess a rifle bullet will fix it," I said.

"The Purple Ones have more power than you know," cried Melvar. "Let us try to get on more open ground before it attacks. Then it will have to leave its cover."

So we turned and ran away from the stream, to a rocky hillside, where the red scrub grew low and scant. As we ran I heard a crashing behind us. Once I turned quickly, and raised my rifle. The strange figure darted abruptly into view, and I fired on the instant. I think I hit it, for it spun around quickly, and fell to the ground. But in a moment it was up, and running toward us with an agility that was incredible, springing over the red brush in great bounds, with a motion more like that of a monstrous hopping insect than of a human being. His white hair was flying in wild disorder, his shrunken limbs plainly flashing purple. And a terrible sound came from it as it bounded along—not a scream of rage or of pain, but a weird uncanny laugh, that rang strangely over the red plain, and somehow made us pause in our race, and tremble with alien terror.

A Narrow Escape

BUT we broke the icy fingers of fear that gripped our hearts, and ran on until we reached a great flat rock that lay at the upper edge of the bare space, in the edge of the thickets again. I lifted Melvar in my arms until she could reach the top and scramble up. Then I looked back and saw the purple man leaping across the clearing with incredible speed, not two hundred yards away.

Then Naro and I got up on that rock—I have never been able to remember just how we did it. I dropped to my knees, seized the rifle that I had pushed up before me, and began to pump lead at the beast as fast as I could work the bolt. The recoils of the gun seemed almost a steady thrust. I heard the bullets thud into the purple body. I saw it checked or driven back by the impacts. One bullet took it off its balance and it fell. But in a moment it was racing on again, empowered by superhuman energy.

When my rifle was empty it was not twenty feet away. One arm was gone. One side of the body was fearfully torn. The purple face was a hideous mangled thing. It did not bleed, but the wounds were covered with a purple viscous slime. One of the eyes was gone, and the other glared at us with a wild red light. Anything of ordinary life must long since have been dead. But it gathered itself, and leapt for the top of the boulder.

On the day before I had showed Melvar how to use my guns, merely by way of proof that there was nothing supernatural in the working of the weapon that had slain so many of the *Astranians* in the temple. Now I pushed one of the pistols toward her. She was standing there motionless, calmly even. There was no panic in her face, and I knew that she would have the courage to use the weapon to save herself from the terrible brute, if things came to the worst. She smiled at me, even as she picked up the gun. Then, looking at the safety, she gripped it in a business-like way.

As the purple monster sprang upon the boulder, I emptied my automatic into it. Great wounds were torn in the dark flesh, and half the face was shot away, but the thing seemed immune to death by ordinary means. As the last shot was fired it stood before us on the rock, a terrible mangled thing, the red eye blazing with demonic inhumanity.

Naro sprang out before me, his crystal sword drawn high. As the beast sprang at him, he cut at it with a mighty sweep of the razor-edged weapon. But the stroke, which would have decapitated an ordinary human, was parried by a terrific blow of the claw-like hand of the thing, and the boy was sent spinning back against me. We fell together on the rock.

Then it hurled itself toward Melvar. It all happened in the briefest of moments, before I could even begin to rise. She swung up the automatic with a quick, sure, graceful movement. She was like a beautiful goddess of battle, with blue eyes shining brightly, and golden hair gleaming in the sun. Again that mad laugh was ringing out, with a choking sob in it, for the thing's vocal organs were injured. It leapt at her, its lacerated limbs working like machines. Calmly she stood, with automatic raised. The muzzle of the gun was not an inch from the throat of the beast when she fired. The strange head was blown completely off the body, and fell rolling and bouncing to the red brush below. The body collapsed, writhing and convulsed. It was not quiet for many minutes.

The girl dropped the gun, suddenly trembling, and threw herself into my arms, sobbing uncontrollably. Her courage and coolness had saved us all, and I admit that I was quite as much unstrung as she after the danger had passed. What a wonderful being she was!

The Red Ship

IT was so late in the day, and we were so completely exhausted that we decided to go no farther. Naro was not hurt, save for a few scratches; and I suppose he was the least excited of the three. In a few minutes he threw the quivering purple body off the boulder and carried it and the head back across the clearing to dispose of them. When he returned we found an overhanging shelf on the north side of the boulder that would afford some shelter from the flying lights. We gathered some of the yellow fruit for supper, cleaned and reloaded the weapons, and prepared to spend the night there.

Naro called me aside and showed me a curious, much-worn silver bracelet, with a singular design upon it. He told me, in his imperfect English, that it had belonged to his father, who had been taken by the flying lights many years before. That was a curious development. It showed that there was some connection between the dreaded Purple Ones, and the terrible, pillaging red lights. But the full significance of it did not dawn upon me until later.

By that time I was in a measure accustomed to the passage of the rushing, whistling needles of crimson fire, and during the first part of the night I was able to sleep, while Naro sat up to keep watch. At midnight he awakened me, and we changed places. The sky was crossed and recrossed by the faint and flickering tracks of red, and the night was weirdly lit by the torpedo-shapes of scarlet flame that sped upon them. With a fatuous sense of security, I was leaning back against the boulder, smoking my pipe and caressing the cold metal of the rifle in my hand, dreaming of what Melvar and I might do if ever we were to emerge into the world alive.

The red thing was upon me before I knew it. The light of my pipe must have been visible to it. In my accursed thoughtlessness, that danger had never occurred to me. The thing came plunging down, flooding the landscape with its lurid crimson radiance, while the earth vibrated to its whistling, hissing scream. There was no need to waken my companions for they sprang to their feet in alarm. We all cowered back against the rock in the hope of escaping observation. But the thing had already seen us.

I put my arm about the warm, throbbing body of Melvar, and drew her close to my breast. Her own cool white hand grasped mine as silently we waited.

The red object came down swiftly, paused just above the crimson thickets before us, then settled deliberately to earth. It was the first opportunity I had had for a close examination of these things. The shape was plainly cylindrical, tapering toward the ends. It was perhaps ten feet in diameter, and a hundred long. Set on the forward end was a bright green globe, perhaps three feet in diameter.

A clump of brush about the end of the cylinder burst into flame. As the bright crimson hue began to dull, I grasped suddenly the fact that the red color was due to the red heat generated by friction with the air, which was very great at the meteor pace the thing attained. It lay there, not fifty yards away, with the fire blazing and crackling about the end on our right, and eating its way into the thickets. The green sphere on the other end seemed to stare at us like a great intent eye. The red color slowly faded. Suddenly Melvar gripped my arm.

"Why wait?" she whispered. "Perhaps it does not see us after all. Let us slip around the boulder."

But on the instant we moved a great oval space swung out of the side of the cylinder. We saw that the door and walls were of a bluish white metal, and were very thick. It was very dark inside. A blood-congealing, eerie laugh sounded out of that darkness, and I shuddered. Quickly five human-like figures leaped one by one out of the oval doorway. With heart-chilling fear, I saw, by the flickering light of the burning thicket that long white hair hanging about faces, wrinkled and hideously aged, with toothless gums, red glaring eyes, and skin that was purple. Without a moment's hesitation, the five naked monsters rushed down upon us.

The fire was fast blazing higher and burning rapidly into the brush between us and the cylinder, and we could see the purple beasts quite plainly in its light. And they were hideous to look upon. They came toward us with monstrous springing bounds, actuated by some extraordinary force. Their muscles must have been far stronger than those of men, perhaps as strongly constructed as those of insects. Or, since muscular force depends on the intensity of nerve currents, perhaps their nerves were extraordinarily excited. And there was something insect-like in the way life had lingered in the body of the one we had killed, when it had already many wounds that should have been mortal.

I leveled my rifle, drew a bead on the neck of the foremost one, and fired. I must have had the luck to shatter the bones, for the head dropped limply to the side. The thing stopped abruptly, groping blindly about with its talon-like fingers. It seemed very strange that it did not fall. In an instant one of the others ran close by it. The crippled monster sprang savagely at the other, and in a moment they were writhing and struggling in the brush, tearing at one another with tiger-like ferocity. The others passed by them for a moment, while I finished emptying the rifle, without visible results.

By that time the crackle of the swiftly spreading fire had grown to a dull roar. It swept fast across the brush, red flames flaring high, and dense smoke rolling up into the night. The purple beasts did not appear to see it. They made no effort to avoid the flames. Were they invulnerable to fire? Or was fire merely unknown to them as to the people of *Astran*?

The three rushed straight on toward us, disregarding the rushing wall of flame not a dozen yards to the right of them. I kept firing madly. The leg of one went limp, but he leapt on with scarcely diminished speed, laughing terribly, with the white hair flying about the awful face, and the purple limbs moving frenziedly. The flames rushed over the fallen two and hid them. In another instant the curtain of fire had rolled over the others, and even the ship was hidden from our view.

Suddenly I realized that we were in quite as much danger from the fire as from the monsters. Already we were shrinking from the hot wind that blew before the flames, and half choked by the acrid fumes. For the second time we made a mad retreat to the top of the boulder, and lay flat. I heard a terrible laugh from the flames, and in a moment one of the things dashed out. His hair was gone, and the purple flesh burnt black. I shot as it showed itself, and it fell. In another instant the flames had raced over it again. None of the others appeared.

We lay on the rock for several minutes, gasping in the cooler air that lingered near its surface. For a time the heat was stifling, but the scanty vegetation had burned off quickly, and soon a cool breeze came up from the south and lifted the smoke. We saw that the cylinder still lay where it had been, although the heavy body was closed. The green light still shone in the forward end. About it the earth lay black and smoking, and a low line of flame lay below the pall of smoke in a great ring all about us. Between us and the ship I saw in the darkness the black shadows that were the five dead beasts.

I was just beginning to wonder if all the crew of the ship were dead, so that we might enter and examine it, when the great oval door in the side swung open again, and something sprang out of it into the night. I heard a strange hissing, and a clatter of metal. In the semi-darkness I could see nothing plainly, but there was a floating shape of greenish mist, with a vague form beneath. I strained my eyes to try to distinguish its shape, while it stood motionless.

Abruptly a narrow, intensely bright beam of orange light shot out of it and impinged upon the rock. There was a dull thud from the rock, and the ray was dead in a moment. But the granite where it had struck was cut away—obliterated! The beam had shone straight through the boulder, carrying away, or resolving into primary electrons, the matter on which it had struck! The smooth edges of the cut were glowing with a soft violet radiance.

My rifle was at hand, and on recovering from my surprise, I fired. I aimed just below the greenish patch. Something must have been exploded by the bullet, for there was a vivid flash of white fire, and a loud, sharp report. The spot of green was visible no longer, and we saw no motion about the cylinder. At the time I had no idea what it was that I had shot. I supposed that it had been another of the purple beasts armed with a strange ray-weapon. I imagined that the bullet had struck the weapon and caused an explosion.

CHAPTER NINE
The Battle in the Mist

FOR perhaps an hour we sat there on the rock. As soon as the smoke cleared, we could see the crimson needles flying high upon their vague red tracks, and we watched them with a sort of hypnotic fascination, dreading the moment when one of them would land to investigate the fate of the ship that lay silent and presumably empty before us. The ground was still too hot for us to walk upon, and we felt the uselessness of attempting to escape on foot, even if it had already cooled. With a feeling of resigned and hopeless horror, we saw one of the crimson pencils circle lower about the place, then disappear in the direction of its lair beyond the Silver Lake.

Even as the whistling roar of its passage was rolling down upon us, Melvar spoke. How I admire the courage and indomitable resourcefulness of the girl. When I was hopelessly lost in despair, feeling all the desolation of this region and the infinite remoteness of the world of men, her pure rich voice and the warm living touch of her hand brought new courage to me.

"The *Krimlu* are coming," she cried. "There is no use to try to fight them, or to try to outrun them. But that ship must be empty. The walls are metal and strong. Perhaps they could not open it."

While there were several things about the proposition that were not very attractive, it seemed our best resource; and, besides, I had a keen desire to see the interior of the thing. We gathered up our equipment, climbed off the boulder, and hurried over to the cylinder. I was possessed by a haunting fear that we would find something hideous awaiting us, but the bright pencil of light from my pocket lamp revealed no living being in the long interior, nor could I find even a trace of the green patch that had blown up in front of the door.

We scrambled through the opening without difficulty and I turned a handle that swung the heavy door shut and evidently locked it.

Then I set about examining the mechanism, for I had an intense curiosity about the propulsive force that enabled the vessel to attain a speed that must have reached thousands of miles per hour. In one end were rows of long cylinders of a transparent substance, evidently filled with the metallic fluid from the Silver Lake. Pipes ran from them to a complex mechanism in the rear end of the ship, from which heavy conduits ran all over the inside of the metal hull. While my understanding of it all was far from complete, I was able to verify a previous idea—that the strange vessels were driven by use of the rocket principle. It seems that the silver fluid was decomposed in the machine, and that the purple gas it formed, at a very high temperature, was forced out through the various tubes at a terrific velocity, propelling the ship by its reaction. The whistling roar of the things in motion was, of course, the sound of the escaping gas, and the red-purple tracks were merely the expelled gas hanging in the air.

The green globe in the forward end may have been the objective lens for a marvelous periscope. At any rate the walls of the forward part of the shell seemed transparent. And the periscope must have utilized infra-red rays, for the scene about us seemed much brighter than it, in reality, was. We could see very plainly the burned plain and the granite rock, and once, through a rift in the clouds of smoke that were rising all about, I caught a glimpse of the gleaming city of *Astran*, high above us in the west.

I noticed a slender lever, with a corrugated disc at the top, rising out of the floor in the bow of the ship. It occurred to me that it was the control lever. I took hold of it and pushed it back. Great jets of purple gas rushed past the transparent walls about us, and the ship slid backward on the ground.

The sensation of motion was most alarming. The illusion of the transparency of the bow of the ship was so perfect that it seemed almost as if we were hanging in space a few feet in front of the mouth of an open tube. It was impossible for me to realize that I was surrounded by solid walls of metal, until I touched them. I think the wonderful telescope worked on much the same principle as television apparatus—that is, that the rays of light were picked up, converted into electrical impulses, amplified, and then projected on the metal wall, which served as a screen.

Battle In the Air

I RETURNED to my experiments with the lever. The control was relatively simple. The vessel was propelled forward when the lever was pushed forward, and reversed when the lever was pulled back. Slipping the little disc up or down raised or lowered the prow, and twisting the thing accomplished the steering in the horizontal plane.

By the time my cautious experiments had revealed all of that Melvar had pointed out three slender crimson craft, wheeling low about us, and evidently preparing to land. I pulled the knob up, and pushed it forward all the way. A pale red beam shot ahead. The black landscape dropped away from us, and we hurtled through the air of the night. I was amazed at the lack of any great sensation of motion, and that the jets of gas, for all their appalling roar without, were barely audible within the cylinder. Still the fore part of the ship was transparent from within, so that we had the oddest sensation of floating free in space.

I saw that the three ships had fallen in a line behind us, and were following at the same terrific pace. When we had reached an altitude of perhaps a mile, I twisted the knob to bring the helm about, and we shot over the Silver Lake, which lay like a white desert of moonlit sand beneath us, standing out sharply against the dark plain around it. In a moment we had gone over it, and over the low hills beyond, and into the bank of purple mist. I had hoped to have time to land and have the vessel on the ground below, but I looked back and saw that our pursuers were gaining swiftly, and that slender twisting rays of bright orange and green were darting toward us from the hurtling arrow-like ships of red.

In the darkness and the mist we could see nothing of the ground below. The only visible things were a few mist-veiled stars above, and the bright scarlet torpedoes that shot after us. Quickly I circled and raised the helm. I was almost intoxicated with excitement, and the indescribable sensations of our swift and lofty flight. I felt released from all the weaknesses of the body; I felt as if I had conquered the force that holds all men to earth. I felt a new and wonderful sensation of freedom and power. I had but to move the little piece of metal in my hand to go where I pleased with the speed, almost, of light. But still came the line of ships behind us, at an incredible pace, stabbing at us with the green and orange rays.

Then, high above the others, I brought the ship around in a hairpin turn, and plunged directly at them. They tried to turn aside, while their rays shot thickly toward us, but our speed was too great. The foremost suddenly turned broadside toward us, attempting to get out of our path. I held our bow directly at it, raised it a trifle at the last instant. The keel of our vessel struck the other amidships. The terrific crash of the collision hurled us to the floor.

When I regained my feet we were falling in a crazy twisting path, our ship altogether out of control. No sooner was I on my feet than the floor tilted up again and I fell back to my hands and knees. I saw that the one we had struck was broken in two and plunging toward the earth far behind us, while the other two were circling about, far overhead. The mist about us grew thicker until the other ships, and the fragments of the wrecked one, were strangely colored purple; thicker still, until they vanished. We floated in a world of purple fog.

I seized the control lever as soon as our wild gyrations enabled me to reach it, but my unskilled efforts only resulted in making us roll and twist more wildly. So long as we had been on an even keel the piloting had been easy enough, although I imagine my success in ramming the other ship had been largely due to luck; but the blow against us had been sidewise, setting the ship to spinning like a top. It seemed that we fell an interminable time. Whenever the stern pointed downward for a moment, I pushed the lever forward, to check our fall as much as possible.

Through the mist I suddenly caught a glimpse of the dark ground below. In another instant the vessel had struck heavily, throwing us against the floor again.

Day was beginning to break at last, and we could see that we had fallen on a bare, gravelly hilltop. The clear space was only an acre or so in extent. We were shut in on all sides by a dense, dark forest of gigantic trees that rose threateningly, seeming to grasp us, to close in on us. The purple mist hung in a sombre curtain overhead, only faintly lighted by the coming day.

The Silver Falls

NARO and I strapped on our packs, picked up our weapons, and opened the door. The three of us stepped out to face the perils of another world. What they might be, we did not know. I had no idea, even, what part of the country was inhabited by the *Krimlu*. But Austen had not let himself be conquered by the mere strangeness of the place. I still hoped to be able to find him, although a search in such a jungle as that about us seemed hopeless.

The walls of the rocket ship were still glowing dully red with the heat of its passage though the air, and we hurried away over the gravel for fifty yards to get beyond the fierce heat it radiated. The patch of sky above was a dull, dusky, luminescent purple. It seemed almost as if the mist shut out the daylight and lit the valley with a weird radiance of its own. All about us towered the forest. As the light grew better, we could see that the trees were red. They bore the same feathery fronds, the same star-like flowers of brilliant white, and the same golden-brown fruits as the plants of the plain about *Astran*. But they were immensely greater; they towered up hundreds of feet. It was like a forest of the tree-ferns of the Carboniferous period, save for the deep bloody scarlet of the leaves. In fact, I think the red plants are descended from some of them, strangely developed by the unusual climatic conditions of the crater, or by the purple mist.

The ground all about the gravelly knoll was low and marshy, and the air was heavy with the odors of rotting vegetation. There was no wind; and the air, under the great atmospheric pressure, was heavy, moist and hot. It was oppressive. It hung like a weight upon our chests. And the crimson jungle seemed to possess a terrible life and spirit of its own. It did not belong to our world.

The undergrowth was very thick. The higher branches were dimmed by the purple mist. They seemed almost to reach the heavy, dull purple sky. It appeared useless to try to penetrate it. It was an evil being waiting to seize us the moment we crossed its bounds.

I got out my compass, and we decided to try to make our way toward the north, in the direction of the pass by which we supposed Austen to have rounded the Silver Lake. As I had last noted our position above the mist, with reference to the lake and the crater walls, we had been about fifteen miles south of the pass, at an estimate. I hoped, by taking a course in that direction, to come across some trace of Austen.

As we approached the north side of the clearing, I made a startling discovery.

In the side of the hill was a deposit of iron pyrites. Not that there was anything remarkable about that. But the thing that struck me was that the vein had been recently worked! I sprang down in the pit and found on the rock traces of copper that had evidently come from soft copper tools. I knew that Austen would have needed minerals, that, indeed, if he had set up a wireless outfit in here, he must have been compelled to do an immense amount of work in collecting and refining the needed materials. I had little doubt that he had been there but it had been evidently weeks or months ago. Any trail that he might have made through the forest would have already grown up.

I thought the situation over for a while, but still there seemed nothing better to do than to follow our original plan of exploring the jungle to the north. We plunged into the crimson gloom. Without the compass we would have been quickly lost. Even with it, it was hard enough to keep in the same direction, walking over the marshy, sodden ground and breaking a path through the heavy undergrowth. We were soon covered with mud and dyed red with the stain of the weird vegetation.

For many hours we struggled through a wilderness of endless sameness—a dank morass, a crimson jungle, with the dusky purple sky hanging heavily in the treetops. The bloody scarlet gloom was startling and terrible.

At first the forest had been quiet, with a silence that was dead and depressing, for there were no living things about us. No birds, no insects—not even a bright moth or butterfly. It was a wilderness of death. But presently we heard, far ahead of us, a dull, constant roar, that grew ever louder as we went on. I supposed that we were approaching a great waterfall. At last it grew so loud that we had to shout when we wished one another to hear our words. I was glad of the roar, for it drowned the sound of our progress through the jungle. But the forest was so dense that there seemed little danger of our capture unless we stumbled unaware on the habitation of the *Krimlu*.

Abruptly the jungle ended, and we stepped out on a bare ledge of stone. Before us was one of the most magnificent spectacles that I have beheld. To the west of us a great black cliff rose perhaps a thousand feet—until it was almost lost against the lowering, smoky purple of the sky. Over it plunged a vast sheet of the glowing white liquid of the Silver Lake, falling in a gigantic unbroken arch to the immense pool beneath us, where it broke, with a deafening roar, into a gleaming bank of soft silver haze. Surrounding the black rock rims of the pool, the gloomy crimson of the forest closed in. The pool was a thousand feet across. The whole scene was colossal; it was awe-inspiring and impressive for the strangeness and intensity of its color.

There was no visible outlet for the silver liquid; so I knew that it must find its way off underground. I knew that we must be far below the level of the Silver Lake and the plain beyond. That fact may have accounted for the more luxuriant growth of the red vegetation.

Suddenly Naro reported the discovery of a comparatively fresh print of a hob-nailed boot in a little patch of mould on the rock. That set us to looking again for traces of Austen, and presently we found a fairly well defined trail that led off to the east. We followed it eagerly. When we had gone a mile we came to an outcropping seam of coal. There I found the plain marks of a copper pick. Evidently a good deal of coal had been dug up and carried off down the trail.

CHAPTER TEN
Austen's Retreat

PERHAPS two hundred yards farther on we came to the camp. It was on a little hilltop below a giant tree. By the trunk was a little mud-daubed hut, with an open shed in front of it. By the shed was a rude clay furnace, with piles of coal, some strange ore, and large lumps of native copper lying by it. Beneath the shed was what appeared to be a small steam turbine, with a kettle like boiler of hammered copper. Connected with it was a dynamo of crude but ingenious construction. Also there was a rude forge, and hammers, anvils, saws and drills, all of copper or bronze, and a device that I supposed had been used for drawing wire.

Simple as it seemed, that camp of Austen's was perhaps the most remarkable thing I came across in the crater. Austen was a wonderful man. Having not only an exhaustive knowledge of a half dozen fields of science—and he had not mere theories, but a practical, working knowledge—he had also courage and determination, patience and manual skill, and a great deal of resourcefulness and invention. While the average man would hardly have been able to keep alive in the jungle, Austen was able to do such things as smelt and refine ore, and set up complicated and workable electrical machinery. Of course he was fortunate in finding himself in a place where practically no effort was needed to satisfy his physical needs, and where he found various natural resources in available and easily accessible form. But I shall never cease to wonder at his accomplishments of less than a year.

I was struck by a sudden fear that we had come too late, and that something had happened to him. "Austen," I shouted, "Austen, are you here?"

For answer, an old man whom I recognized joyfully as the old scientist appeared in the rude doorway of the hut. His clothing was tattered beyond description, and he looked very worn and thin. There were lines of age—and care about his wrinkled face. But his hair was neatly brushed, and he had just been shaving, for his safety razor was in his hand. A smile of astonishment and incredulous joy sprang over his face. For a moment he was speechless. Then the old familiar voice called out uncertainly, almost sobbing with joy.

"Winfield! Melvar! Naro! Can it really be you? At last!"

Then, as if he were a little ashamed of the feeling he had shown, he pulled out his pipe and began to try to fill it, his fingers trembling with emotion. But Melvar sprang to him and threw her arms about him in a way that gave me a momentary pang of jealousy. He stuck the pipe back in his pocket, grinning awkwardly, in a way that tightened the strings of my heart.

"I forgot," he said. "My tobacco was all gone a week ago."

I shook his hand, and it clung to mine for a moment as if he were seeking support. Then Naro placed his palm upon Austen's shoulder in the customary greeting of *Astran*.

"I'd almost given up," the old man said. "The world is so far away that it seems almost unreal. After I had sent the wireless call a few times the devilish rustling in the sky got too close for comfort, and I decided that the hissing red lights, whatever they are, were about to locate me by the signals. So I quit that. But how did you come over?"

I told him briefly about the adventure with the red ship.

"Yes, I knew that the things were ships of some kind," he said when I had finished. "I have been working on the quicksilver stuff, and making a few exploring trips. I have discovered several things. I had to work—to work endlessly—to keep going. Sometimes I got to feeling pretty low. Then I would shave, and try to clean up like a civilized man. And I kept repeating all the poetry I knew—that helped a lot. But Lord—you haven't any idea how glad I am to see you. By the way, did you bring the spectroscope and tubes?"

By way of reply, I took off the pack that contained them. He began to open it with as much enthusiasm as a small boy investigating a Christmas present. Suddenly he paused and looked at us. "But you don't look like you've had any holiday yourselves. What has happened to you?"

"Two or three things," I told him. "It hasn't been a holiday at all. Do you happen to have any coffee left? I left mine in the tent outside the cliffs."

"And how about a little hot Mulligan stew to go with it?" he grinned, beckoning the way inside.

The Scientist Speaks

SO we went into the cabin. Most of the room seemed to be devoted to his crude laboratory equipment. On one of his benches were several roughly modeled pottery jars, filled with the liquid from the Silver Sea. His bunk was in a screened off corner.

In a few minutes he had the coffeepot boiling over a charcoal brazier. I believe that aroma is about the most pleasant that ever reached my nostrils. I was too much absorbed in it to do much talking, but Melvar sat down on one of Austen's rustic stools and gave him an account of our adventures.

When the coffee was done, Austen served a meal consisting in addition of a great pot of steaming soup made of the yellow fruits cooked with the tender roots of the red plants. That stands out in my memory as one of the truly magnificent repasts that have ever been laid before me.

When we had finished Melvar retired to Austen's bunk, and Naro and I lay down on a blanket on the laboratory floor. I went to sleep at once, and, if I may credit the word of our host, slept for thirty-seven and a half hours. Although I am inclined to believe that is an exaggeration.

At any rate, when I got up, I felt a new man. Austen had set up the apparatus we brought. He had a test tube full of the silver liquid set up in a beam of X-rays, and the spectroscope in position to examine the dense purple gas that was rising from the stuff.

"How is it coming?" I asked him.

He shook his head sadly. "I don't know," he said. "I have a theory, but it doesn't seem to work out right. The key is in sight but it always eludes me. There is energy stored in the silver liquid. It may be that that amazing thing in the sky stores the energy of sunlight in the stuff. You know that the energy in sunlight amounts to something over one horsepower for each square yard on which it falls. Or perhaps the atomic energy of the gases in the air is released. It seems impossible to find the key, although I have been able to analyze the stuff pretty accurately. If I had it I could make the silver stuff go off like ten times its weight of T.N.T."

"Do you think," I asked him eagerly, "that you could set off some of it and wipe out the *Krimlu?*"

"Winfield," the old scientist soberly replied, "even if you could, would you wipe out a whole civilization—a science so high as that which made the Silver Lake—a culture equal to, if not above, that of our own world?"

"If you had seen those purple things—men and women that are old and hideous, and fearfully strong, and malignant—you couldn't move too quickly to blot them off the earth," I cried.

"I have seen," he said seriously. "I have seen the purple monsters, and they are terrible enough. But they are not the masters. They are but the servants, or perhaps I should say the machines, of a higher power. I told you that I had been exploring a bit. I have seen some strange things.

"There is another form of intelligence here, Winfield. A form of life unrelated to humanity, without any sympathy for mankind, for any share of human feelings. Perhaps it is a danger to the human race. The things would not hesitate, I suppose, to use all humanity as they have used the people of *Astran*. But that does not solve the problem. Would it be right to wipe them out? Perhaps it would be better for mankind to go under. Perhaps they are superior to us. The purposes of the creation of intelligent life might be better met by these things than by man. I have given it a great deal of thought, and I can't decide."

He fell silent and presently I said, "You say there is another form of life here. What is it like?"

"You will know soon enough. I wish I had never seen. It is not a good thing to talk about. There is no use for me to tell you."

The Chasm of the Strange Machine

HE would tell me no more. Presently I left him and went down to bathe in the stream of water that flowed back of the camp. The water was sluggish and tepid, certainly not invigorating, but it was cleansing. When I got back Melvar and Naro were up. The girl had been very glad to see Austen again. She was talking with him, very vivacious, and very beautiful. When I saw her, I loved her, if possible more than ever.

As soon as we had eaten, Austen began to dismount the spectrometer and other equipment, and to pack them. "I can go no farther with the experiments here," he said. "I am going to take the outfit to a place where we can see one of the engines of the *Krimlu*, where the silver liquid is broken up. There I may be able to get the clue I need."

In an hour we were ready to depart. Austen led the way, silent and preoccupied with the details of his work. We went down a narrow trail through the stagnating marshes, in the eldritch gloom of the weird red jungle, under the dull purple mist. For many hours we were on the way, until the purple dusk began to thicken, and a distant sighing whistle told us that night had fallen, and that the evil masters were abroad again.

Suddenly Austen called out in a guarded tone for us to halt. We all crept forward cautiously until we could see over the brink of a vast circular chasm. Sheer black walls, ringed by the red jungle, fell for a thousand feet. The round floor was a half mile across. Upon it was the most gigantic and amazing mechanical device I have ever seen. The thing was incredibly huge, and throbbing with strange energy. It made little sound, but the space about us seemed vibrant with power.

In the center of the pit was a titanic, shining green cylinder, perhaps a hundred feet in diameter and five hundred in length. A river of gleaming silver fluid ran from an opening in the rock, through a great open aqueduct, and poured into the cylinder in the middle of the upper side. At each end of the colossal cylinder rose a metal tower. At the top of each tower was a fifty-foot globe of blue crystal, slowly turning. Between and above the spheres arched a high-flung span of white fire—a great pulsing sheet of milky opalescent light—that roared and crackled like a powerful electric discharge, and lit the chasm with an unearthly radiance.

Toward the farther side of the floor was a second enormous machine, apparently unconnected with the first, resembling a vast telescope. The white metal tube was a full two hundred feet in length, mounted on massive metal supports. It did not seem to be in action. The barrel of it was pointing at the sky, like a telescope, or a cannon.

Then I saw a row of openings low down in the side of the vast green cylinder, with shafts of bright green light pouring from them. And I saw tiny human figures working feverishly about them. They had escaped my observation at first, so far away was the floor of the pit. Now I saw that they were taking great blocks of a luminous green substance from the doors in the cylinder and carrying them to the tube that was pointing at the sky.

I saw now that the bodies of the toilers were purple. There was something in their motion that reminded me of ants. I was amazed at their strength and agility, at their ceaseless, machinelike activity. They never looked about, never paused, never rested. They were like machines, or animated corpses, driven to endless toil by some strange force. I remembered the time I had splashed the white fluid on my arm, turning it purple, and the strange excitement of my nerves. At once I linked up the raids on *Astran,* the bracelet that Naro had found on the dead purple beast, and what Austen had told me of superior beings who enslaved the purple things. I knew that I looked upon the captured men and women of *Astran,* simply *man-machines* in this strange place!

Perhaps they were already dead. Certainly they moved, not by their own volition, but by a stronger mechanical power. They must have been under the absolute hypnotic control of the higher intelligences, who treated their unfortunate captives, perhaps with the argent liquid, to convert them into unearthly machines of super-human strength.

We turned away into the night that had fallen on the red jungle while we watched. I was sick with horror. Austen's face was white and his hands were trembling. There was a stern, fierce light in his eye. Now I knew, in spite of what he had said, that were the opportunity given him, he would not hesitate to wipe out the masters of the purple slaves. He said nothing, but his hands worked spasmodically, he muttered under his breath, and his dark eyes snapped with angry determination.

In a few minutes we set about preparing the apparatus for the work of the night. The spectroscope was set up, with telescopic condensers, to collect and analyze the radiation of the arch of crackling milky flame. We took care to screen ourselves in the jungle fringe, and to expose no more of the equipment to the sight of the beings below than was necessary. Austen had his drawing board set up in a convenient place behind our shelter, and he alternately peered through the telescope at the spectrum, and turned to make intricate calculation in the light of a shaded flashlight. We sat up all night at the work.

All night long the white flame played between the spinning blue crystal spheres above the vast green cylinder, filling the air with its ghostly crackle and whisper. All night long the tireless purple human machines toiled in the pit, carrying the great green blocks, and evidently stacking them in the vast cannon-like tube at the side. Whenever Austen did not need me with the analysis, I spent the time searching that amazing scene, but not once did I catch a glimpse of anything that might have been the directing intelligence of all that marvelous activity.

Melvar had been very tired, and I had contrived a hammock for her from a great sheet of fibrous bark torn from the trunk of one of the red trees. She spent the night asleep in that, while Austen and I carried on the work, and Naro, not having scientific inclinations, contented himself with a couch composed of a few feathery branches torn from the undergrowth.

CHAPTER ELEVEN
What the Analysis Showed

JUST before daylight Austen completed his calculations, and stated the result. He was very tired, and his eyes were red. He had worked for a day and two nights since we had found him. He gave his conclusion in a colorless monotone.

"You know," he said, "that there are several rare gases in the air, in addition to oxygen and nitrogen. The inert gas argon comprises nearly one percent of the atmosphere, and there are, in addition, smaller quantities of helium, neon, xenon, and krypton, not to mention the carbon dioxide and water vapor. Those gases are monatomic and do not ordinarily enter into any compounds at all.

"You know that lightning in the air causes a union of nitrogen and oxygen, to form nitrous and nitric acids, which may later release their energy in the explosion of gun powder or nitroglycerine. In much the same way the force that forms the silver fluid utilizes the photochemical effect of sunlight to build up a complex molecule containing oxygen, nitrogen, and the inert gases of the helium group. It is very unstable, and may be disrupted with the release of a great amount of energy. I was able to detect the characteristic lines of most of the gases in the luminous spectrum of the purple gas, but not until I had analyzed the light of the opalescent flame, and made my deductions from that, was I able to derive the equations and arrive at the precise structural formula, and at the exact wave length necessary to break down the molecule."

He proceeded to launch into a detailed technical discussion of the process of analysis he had used, and of the methods of inductive reasoning by which he had arrived, at his conclusion. It was rather deep for me, and I am afraid some of the salient points have already slipped my mind. But

I doubt that the general reader would be interested in it anyhow.

Something more important was on my mind.

"Have you found out enough?" I asked. "Can you blow up the stuff? Can you wipe out the *Krimlu?*"

"I am not sure," he said, "but I think, if I could get at that machine with a little of my equipment I could manipulate it to make it go off like a thousand tons of dynamite. The silver stuff runs into the cylinder and is converted into pure vibrant energy. If I could just speed up the process a bit!

"The *Krimlu* seem to live underground like ants. A month ago I found an opening into their world near the cliffs, south of the fall. There are the shafts where their ships come out, ventilator tubes, and funnels for the purple smoke from their engines. I will go down one of the shafts and see what can be done."

"You mean *we* will go," I told him. "You don't think—"

"There is no need for you to risk your life," he said in a voice purposely brusque to hide his emotion. "I can do as much by myself. Then there is Melvar. We must get her out of here if we can. I think a great deal of her. If we both should go—and not come back— No, I want you to stay on top. I know I can trust you to treat her fairly. If I can blast down the earth on their underground world, we might be able to make it back around the Silver Sea, and eventually to the outside."

"You can trust me, sir, to care for her to the best of my ability," I told him, looking at the sandal on my right foot, and trying, without notable success, to keep my voice even and casual.

"*Really*," he cried, looking at me intensely, "do you love her?"

I ADMITTED that I did, even using, as I remember the occasion, rather an enthusiastic, if hackneyed phrase to describe my feeling.

"I had hoped so," Austen said. "She and you are the dearest ones to me in the world. If you were out and safe, I could—go—in peace."

The rude hammock in which Melvar had been lying sprang into violent motion and erupted her slender, beautiful figure. She came running toward me. "I am sorry," she gasped. "No, I mean I am glad. I was awake, Winfield. I heard you—" Her farther statements were not particularly coherent, since she was kissing me, and I was holding her in my arms and returning the gesture. I gathered on the whole that my feelings for her were well reciprocated. Some minutes later, when I came back to earth, I observed that Austen was taking the equipment down, and that Naro was standing and looking at us with an expression of extreme and comical disgust on his frank and boyish face.

By that time it was light, and soon, by the brightening of the purple haze above, we knew that the sun was rising. I saw that Austen was looking into the pit. Melvar ad I walked to the edge. The great metal tube, which tired purple beings had been all night in loading with the green bars, was being swung slowly about upon its mounting, until presently it was pointing at the sky above the Silver Sea.

For a moment nothing happened; then a low, deep, humming drone reached our ears, coming apparently from the complex machinery at the base of the tube. Steadily the sound rose in pitch, until it was an intolerably high and painful scream. Suddenly, when the high rhythm of it had become unsupportable, we ceased to hear it; but I knew that it had merely passed up the scale beyond the range of our ears, and was sounding still.

Abruptly the colossal tube seemed to flash into green incandescence and a broad beam of yellow light, blindingly brilliant, and pulsing with strange energy, poured up into the dusky purple sky. Then I knew that it was this machine that made the amazing thing above the Silver Sea, from which the white liquid fell.

As we watched, bright patches of red and green shot up the beam. Slowly the bright yellow faded from the ray, but still the green luminosity clung about the tube, and still I felt that the flood of radiant, purposeful energy was flowing up into the sky. It was not long before I heard, far above us, in the distant west beyond the red-clad hill, the splash of the first great drop of silver into the argent lake. Below us the white torrent was still pouring into the vast green cylinder, the white fire was still arching between the crystal globes, and the purple slaves were still rushing about the pit with feverish and machine-like energy.

We turned away from the place and walked back into the terrible and weird semi-darkness of the scarlet jungle, still beneath the shadow of the evil intelligence that ruled the crater. I had the knowledge of Melvar's love, and the bright charm of her nearness, but I felt the unholy power of the jungle already closing about to crush us.

We reached the camp long before night, and Austen and I went to sleep. The old scientist was up again at daylight. I was amazed at his energy and vitality. He got ready the equipment he intended to take, as we were soon ready to set out for the entrance of the underworld. Austen insisted that we leave Melvar and Naro behind. There was no use, he said, to expose them to the hardships and dangers of the journey, and it seemed that no harm would be likely to come to them at the cabin. Then, without them, we could travel faster and with less danger of detection. I did not like to leave Melvar, but she was very courageous about it, smiling through her tears. It always takes more courage in those who stay behind and wait than for those who have the lure of mystery and adventure to beckon them on.

Melvar walked with me to the edge of the clearing, and there we left her, taking a dim trail that led through the dense jungle to the south. Austen was saying nothing. He was lost in meditation. But I knew that when the time came for action, he would lose no time in thought. But how could I guess the noble thoughts that were passing in his mind? How could I realize that he was marching willingly to his doom? For my part, I was thinking of the wonderful girl I had left at the cabin. I thought, too, of the horror of the lights that haunted *Astran*, and of the horror that would be if the lights ever went beyond the rim—into the outer world.

After several hours Austen stopped. "It is not a half mile to the shafts," he said. "We shall have to make a rope. I have made cords from the tough bark of the red trees. That does very well. I want to reach the bottom of the pit before night. But I have reason to think that the things are active in their underworld at all hours of the day, emerging only at night because the magnetic vibration of sunlight interferes with the operation of the delicate machinery of their bodies." Of that, I came to a better understanding later.

We began to weave a rope of strips of leather-like bark torn from the mighty red trees. We kept at it until we had many hundred feet of the tough strands. As we worked Austen began to talk a little, in a voice that was very low, and a little husky, of his boyhood on a Western farm, and of the bright spots of his life. He told a few stories of his school and college days, and of the girl he had loved and lost. But when the rope was finished and coiled, he fell silent again, and grimly examined his automatic. He adjusted his pack, got out his pipe and filled it with my tobacco, and grinned. Then he said soberly, "We are here. We are ready to play our hand, to win or to lose. And if we lose—"

He thrust out his hand. I shook it and we walked on silently. We had now gone more than a hundred yards when the scarlet forest thinned, and we walked out on a level stretch of bare white sand. The clear space was perhaps a mile long and half as wide. Along the western side rose a dark precipitous cliff, like that over which the silver fall plunged, with a line of red brush along the top. At the foot was a great sloping bank of talus, scattered with gigantic boulders. The cliff and the lofty crimson forest that rimmed the open space on the other three sides, seemed to reach into the dusky purple of obscurity of the low-hanging sky.

Spaced irregularly about the center of the flat were perhaps a dozen low circular metal structures—evidently the mouths of great white metal tubes projecting from the earth. From five of them dense clouds of purple vapor were pouring.

The Sacrifice

WE left the shelter of the jungle and quickly approached the nearest of the wells. The metal curbing was about four feet high, around a circular pit some 20 feet in diameter. We leaned over and looked into it. The tube was lit faintly for a few feet down the walls, but we saw no light toward the bottom of the tube. A faint humming sound came up out of the darkness, and I felt a strong current of air flowing down the tube. It was altogether stranger and more terrible than I had anticipated. I doubt that I could have found the courage to descend.

"Is the rope long enough?" I whispered.

"Yes," he replied in a cautious undertone. "On the day I discovered the place I dropped a pebble in the well and timed its fall with my watch. The depth is just over five hundred feet."

I put the end of the cord over the metal rim and paid it out until only enough was left to hitch around my body. With a smile of forced cheerfulness, Austen looked to his pack, knocked out the pipe, and put it in his pocket.

"Winfield, my boy, I hope to see you soon again," he said. "It may take only an hour or two to lay my mine and return to the shaft. But of course I know nothing of what I am to encounter. You wait and hold the rope, and if I need to send you any message I will jerk it three times, and you can pull it up. The note will tell when to put it down again for me to climb out. Good-by, my boy. You——"

He started to say something more, but his voice broke, and he turned abruptly to the well. I braced myself against the curbing, and he climbed over and started down. I looked over and watched him. In a few moments his head and shoulders had shrunk to a little blot against the darkness of the well. Soon he was out of my sight, although for a long time I felt the tugging of the rope. Suddenly the tension relaxed. He had reached the bottom, or—fearful thought!— he had lost his grip on the rope and was hurtling downward through the darkness. I listened in an agony of suspense. It was several minutes before I was reassured to feel three twitches of the cord. I pulled it up. On the end was tied a piece of paper, with these words penciled upon it:

"Dear Winfield, I hate to leave us thus, without telling you, as I intend to do. But I could not tell you. Go back, get Melvar, and travel as far as you can from this accursed place. May you and she survive and lead a happy life together, in here if you cannot reach the world beyond.

"I will give you twenty hours. In that time you can go far north of the silver fall. I am sure, with the equipment I have with me, I can explode one of the engines and send all this part of the valley skyward—if I live to carry out my plan.

Good-by, Austen."

Then I saw that he had been planning all along to give up his life. The note had been written some time before he left. I cursed the stupidity that had kept me from perceiving his intention. If I had but thought, I would have known it was impossible for the aged scientist to climb the rope from the bottom of the pit. Dear old Austen! The truest friend I ever had! His wrinkled, smiling face, his kind blue eyes, his low familial voice, are gone forever!

CHAPTER TWELVE
The Forest Aflame

I HAVE a very confused recollection of what happened immediately afterward. My own actions seem a vague, disordered dream. My bitter grief at Austen's self-sacrifice was the only thing real to me. I believe I began carrying rocks from the boulder-strewn slope at the foot of the cliff, with the idea of securing the rope to them so I could go down in search for him. But my memory of that is very faint.

The first thing I remember clearly is that I was staggering back to the shaft with a heavy rock in my arms, when I caught a whiff of acrid smoke and awoke to the realization that the purple sky was darkened with drifting clouds, and the air was already heavy with the suffocating pungent odor of the burning red vegetation. My instinctive alarm at the thought of fire served to bring me to myself, and I was suddenly fearful for the safety of Melvar.

I knew that, had the red-hot rocket ship in which we had crossed the Silver Sea chanced to fall in the jungle instead of on the barren hilltop, a conflagration would have spread from it at once. Abruptly I remembered that the glowing fragments of the one we had wrecked had fallen in the northern forest. Austen's cabin lay in that direction! I knew that the red vegetation was peculiarly inflammable, and that the fire fed on the oxygen of the heavy atmosphere, would advance with terrible speed.

For a moment, in a panic of indecision, I listened. From the north I heard the crackling roar of a mighty conflagration. Then my mind was made up. Any attempt to find Austen and induce him to give up his plan of self-sacrifice would be terribly uncertain. Melvar was in immediate danger, and I knew that Austen valued her life above his own. But even then, I knew in my heart that it was too late, though I would not let myself believe it. Fire is a pitiless and remorseless enemy.

At a dead run I started up the trail by which we had entered the clearing. Ever the smoke became thicker and more acrid, while the crackling roar of the fire rang ever louder in my ears. I ran on through the ghastly gloom of the scarlet jungle, in made desperation, even after hope was gone, until the hot suffocating breath of the flames was choking me, until the bright lurid curtain of the fire was spread before my eyes, and the intense heat radiation blistered my skin. The vast wall of flame swept forward like a voracious demoniac thing of crimson, implacable, irresistible, overwhelming. It plunged forward like a rushing tidal wave of red. *Already the fire had passed the site of the cabin!*

I was suddenly hopeless, and despairing, and very tired. The flames rushed forward faster, by far, than a human being could force a way through the jungle. With the knowledge that I had just lost the only two beings that in all the world of men ever mattered to me, it hardly seemed worth while to try to save my own life. For a moment I stood there, about to cast myself into the flames. But it is not the nature of an animal to die willingly, no matter how slight the promise of life may be.

When I could endure the heat no longer, when the pain of my blistered skin, and the outcries of my tortured lungs had grown unsupportable, I turned and ran toward the clearing again. Behind me, the flames roared like a lightning express. The fern-like fronds burned explosively, like gun-cotton. My nostrils and lungs were seared and smarting. The hot wind dried my skin and left it scorched and cracked. I was blinded by the smoke. I longed to throw myself down and seek the temporary ecstasy of a breath of clear air from near the ground, of a cooling plunge into a muddy pool. The red jungle reeled about me, but I fought my way on, like a man in a dream.

At last I staggered into the open space. The last of the giant trees exploded into flames not a score of yards behind me. Sparks rained upon me. My clothing caught fire. I ran on, fighting at it with my hands. The jungle back of me roared deafeningly, an angry, surging sea of lurid red flames, awful, overwhelming, fantastically terrible. Heat radiation poured across the clearing in a pitiless beam. I struggled on across the white sand away from flames that tossed themselves up like volcano-ridden ranges of scarlet alps, until I reached the shelter of a great boulder on the slope below the cliff.

I flung myself down behind the rock, gulping down the cool air and rubbing out the fire in my clothing with my blackened hands. For many hours I lay there, tortured by thirst and pain. At last I fell into a light sleep of troubled dreams, in which huge, winged, green ants flew after me through burning crimson forests and in which I saw the dear form of Melvar devoured again and again by the flames.

I was awakened, after a time, I know not how long, by a cool wind that had sprung up from the north. For a moment my mind was lost in blank wonder, and then came the desolate memory that Melvar and Austen were lost. In hopeless misery I got weakly to my feet and walked unsteadily around the boulder until I could look across the clearing.

As I leaned against the rock, gazing eastward, it was a strangely altered and desolate scene that lay before my eyes. The red forest was gone. Below me was a region of low rolling hills, black and grim beneath the lowering, smoky purple sky. The white sand about me stood out in sharp contrast to the charred and gloomy waste beyond, from which a few slender wisps of dark smoke were still rising. All life was gone. It was a dead world. But still the dense purple clouds poured out of the shafts of the underworld, adding their weight to the dismal sky.

A great homesickness for the world, and my fellow men came over me. Then I heard a strange humming behind me, and a slight metallic clatter. I turned around in apathetic curiosity.

A Strange Duel

AND I came face to face with a monster so utterly strange and weirdly terrible that the very shock of it almost unseated my wandering reason. But so completely had my interests and hopes in life been severed, so near was I to the great divide of death that I was past emotion of any kind. At first I looked on the thing with a curious lack of interest, as the soul of one newly dead might look with numbed faculties on his new habitation. But as I looked upon it, an icy current of fear stole over me like the creeping cold of the north, and clasped me to its frozen breast. I had met so many horrors that I had begun to think myself immune to terror. But I had met no such thing as that.

I knew that it was an intelligent, a sentient being. But it was not human, not a thing of flesh and blood at all. It was a machine! Or, rather, it was in a machine, for I felt far more of it than I saw—a will, a cold and alien intellect, a being, malefic, inhuman, inscrutable. It was a thing that belonged, not in the present earth, but in the tomb of the unthinkable past, or beyond the wastes of interstellar space, amid the inconceivable horrors of unknown spheres.

There was a bright, gleaming globe, three feet in diameter, lit with vivid flowing fires of violet and green. A strange swirling mist of brilliant points of many colored lights danced madly about it—a coruscating fog of iridescent fire—moving, flickering, in an incredible rhythm.

That unearthly thing rested upon a frame of metal. It was the head of a metallic monster. It was set on an oblong box of white metal, to which were attached six long-jointed metal limbs. The being stood nine feet high, at least. It was standing on three of the limbs and holding my rifle, which I had left where I had been lying, turning it and feeling of it with a cluster of slender, fingerlike tentacles on the end of the metal arm. It was working the mechanism of the gun, and apparently looking at it, though it had no eyes that I could see.

Suddenly the gun went off, throwing up the sand between me and the monster. With a grotesquely half-human attitude of alarmed surprise, the being dropped the gun and sprang back like a gigantic spider. The motion freed me from my paralysis of horror, and I started backing cautiously around the boulder, afraid to run. As I moved it sprang forward and a slender tube of white metal, in one of the tentacled hands, was suddenly pointed toward me. As the monster moved, there was a humming sound from it, and little jets of purple gas hissed from holes in the sides of the box-like body.

I drew my automatic and fired at the metal tube. I must have made an unusually fortunate shot, for the object was carried out of the metal grasp, and fell spinning on the sand. On the instant, I turned and ran toward another great boulder, as large as a railroad locomotive that lay fifty yards to the north. As I ran I heard the clatter and whirring of the mechanical being. I paused at the edge of the rock and took a last glimpse back.

The monster was holding the little tube in one of its limbs, and apparently adjusting it with another. Then it suddenly extended the thing toward me. I dived behind the rock. And a bright ray of orange light shot past the boulder—a beam like that which had come from the being in the door of the rocket ship. Then I knew that here was an entity of the same kind as the one I had destroyed that night—one of the ruling intelligences of the crater, the *Krimlu*.

For several minutes I crouched behind the boulder, expecting the terrible being to come striding around after me at any instant; but it did not come, so presently I began to think. Perhaps the things were not so powerful, or so extremely intelligent after all. I had killed one, even if it was just by a chance shot in the dark. This one had seemed surprised and alarmed when the rifle went off, and I supposed that a being so intelligent as I had at first thought it to be might have inferred the nature and use of the weapon from its appearance. And I thought that it must be afraid of me, after my pistol bullet had knocked its own weapon out of its grip, or it would have followed me around the boulder. Then I began to wonder what it was going to do.

It evidently intended to strike me with the ray weapon. And not only did it respect me, but it knew that I stood in deathly fear of it. It knew that I was trying to escape, so it might reasonably expect me to leave the unscalable cliff and attempt a break against the open country. And if I were to do that, I would naturally keep in the shelter of my own boulder as long as possible. If the monster thought in that way, the logical thing for it to do would be to creep out of the upper side of its rock, where I would inevitably come into its sight by whatever direction I left my breastwork.

Of course there was a frightful risk in taking any action on such a hypothesis—a greater risk than I realized at the time. If the monster were less intelligent than I supposed, I might blunder on it; if it were more intelligent, it might have anticipated my plan—might be waiting to trap me.

But I crawled out along the upper side of my boulder and peered over a smaller rock, which would serve me as a breastwork, my automatic ready. I expected to see the creature in my range, and itself intent upon my other lines of retreat. But it was not there. For a moment I thought I was doomed, but the orange ray did not strike, and I was forced to the conclusion that the monster was not in a position for action at all.

For a moment I was tempted to precipitate flight across the clearing, but I knew that such a move would put me at the mercy of the ray, and I thought that it might not yet be too late to carry out my original plan. I lay flat, with the gun trained on the spot where I expected it to appear. For perhaps fifteen minutes nothing happened; then it proved that my hypothesis was justified. The weird being suddenly sprang into view, with the strange weapon grasped in its glittering arm. It seemed to be looking beyond my boulder. I was lying ready, with the automatic leveled. It was a matter of the merest instant to aim at the green sphere and pull the trigger.

The globe was shattered as if it had been made of glass. The glittering fragments showered off the metal box, while the whole mechanical body suddenly became very rigid, and fell heavily to the side. A puff of coruscating green mist floated out of the globe as it broke, and swiftly dissipated, and the sparkling lights were about the thing no more. The monster was evidently dead.

For a few long moments I hesitated, but I was sure the thing had been killed, and my curiosity got the better of my fear. I cautiously approached it. For a moment I stood marveling at the wonderful workmanship of the machine and at the cleverness of its design; then I saw something that made me forget all else. Something beside the crystal shell had fallen.

The tissue of it was very delicate, and it had been broken by the fall, so that the body juices were running from it. Its brain cavity was very large—perhaps even larger than that of a man—covered only with a thin chitinous shell. The limbs were but thin tentacles, almost altogether atrophied. In fact, the brain appeared to be about three-fourths of the total bulk. The body was so badly smashed that I really could tell little about it, but the tiny limbs were covered with chitin, and there were the rudimentary stumps of fine, tissue-like wings. There were no visible traces of digestive organs, or of mandibles.

The thing was plainly an insect of some kind. From just what species it had sprung in the long process of evolution in the crater it would be most difficult to say. For several reasons, I believe it was an ant. At any rate, it had reached about the ultimate stage of evolution. Machines had altogether replaced bodies of flesh and blood. I believe the thing had been nourished by the sparkling green vapor, which must have circulated like blood through the protecting crystal sphere.

It seems incredible to find great intelligence in any form of life other than human; but science thinks that life and intelligence must rise and fall in recurring cycles, and that the earth has probably been ruled by many different forms of life, each of which has been blotted out by some cataclysm. The *Krimlu* were a surviving remnant of archaic ages.

CHAPTER TWELVE
When Austen Struck

I LOST little time in the examination of the dead creature. The shafts from which it had come were but a few hundred yards below, and the purple gas was still rolling out of the funnels. I did not know when a second monster might follow the first. My mind was too much upset by grief and terror to be capable of intelligent planning, but I knew I wanted to get away from here, and I think I had some notion of reaching the northern pass, and of getting back to an unburned growth of the red vegetation, for I was weak with thirst and hunger. But all that was very vague.

I walked around the wells, keeping at a distance; and struck out for the east as fast as my wearied limbs could carry me. Soon the cliff was out of sight. All about was the desolate, rolling black landscape, with the gloomy purple sky overhead. My thoughts were as dark and sere as the world. Memories of dear old Austen and of lovely Melvar were always with me, even when I tried to banish them and to think rationally of my position.

When I had gone perhaps three hours from the cliff, and had almost lost my fear of pursuit, I saw a great cigar-shaped object of gleaming white on a low hill before me. So dulled were my perceptions that it was many minutes before I realized that it was the rocket ship in which we had come over the Silver Sea. Then, bringing a faint thrill of hope, the thought came to me that it was still probably in a condition to fly, and that, if I could succeed in controlling it, it offered a possible avenue of escape from the crater.

I walked up to the thick metal walls. They seemed undamaged by the fire. Of course, they were used to withstanding the far higher temperatures developed during flight. I walked around the ship, and was surprised to see that the heavy metal door, which we had left open, had been swung shut. Lying against it was the charred skeleton of a man. About the bones were woven metal garments and crystal armor that I recognized with a shock as Naro's. So, I thought, the fellow had deserted his beautiful sister to seek the shelter of the rocket ship, and had fallen a victim to the flames at the last moment.

For a moment, I stared grimly at the remains; then, animated by a sudden ray of hope, I sprang to the door, pulled it open, and leaped into the ship. There, lying on the floor, was the lovely form of Melvar. Her clothing was tattered and smeared with stains of red and black from the burning forest, but she was unharmed. It was almost incredible to me to find her restored. I was half afraid that my mind had failed at last, and that she was but—an illusion. I dropped on my knees beside her, and kissed her warm red lips. She stirred a little and, still but half awake, put a trustful arm about my shoulder.

"Winfield, I knew you would come," she whispered at last. "But where are Naro and Austen?"

"They will never come," I said.

She drew me fiercely toward her, as if to use me for a shield against the awful truth. It was some time before she was able to talk; but presently she told me how Naro had seen the smoke, and how she had thought of seeking shelter from the fire in the rocket ship. They had run down the trail we had made as we left the ship. The fire had overtaken them just as they reached it. The boy had carried her the last few yards, had put her through the door, and then had been unable to enter himself. But, a hero to the last, a worthy warrior of old *Astran*, he had swung the door shut with his dying motion.

Presently I turned my attention to the ship. The marvelous periscope still gave the illusion that the bow was transparent. When I moved the little control lever, the jets of purple gas rushed out again. After a time I had the vessel worked loose from its place in the earth. Then, once again, I pulled up the little metal knob and pushed it forward.

The blackened terrain was colored by the purple mist. It was dimmed, blurred, blotted out. We shot through the purple cloud and abruptly plunged into clear air and blessed sunshine. Melvar stood by me, with her arm upon my shoulder. She cried out gladly as we came into the light. It was not quite noon and the sun was shining very brightly into the crater. The crescent Silver Lake was still gleaming with the same argent luster, and *Astran* shone like a great gem set in the dark red upland beyond.

Suddenly the clouds of purple mist below were thrown up and scattered in a thousand ragged streamers. A great blaze of opalescence burst out where it had been. A flood of fire ran over the Silver Sea. It was a white, milky light like that we had seen between the blue crystal globes of the great machine in the chasm. In a moment the whole crater was a torn and angry ocean of iridescent flame. The red upland was blotted out, and *Astran* vanished forever. White flames that were like the tongues of burning hydrogen that burst from exploding suns, flared up behind us.

Then we heard the sound of the cataclysm—a crashing roar like the thunder of a thousand falling mountains, as deep, as vast, as awful, as the crash of colliding worlds. At the same instant we felt the force of the greatest explosion that has ever occurred on earth. The rocket shot upward as though shot out of a mighty cannon. The blue sky darkened about us, and the stars flamed out like a million scintillating gems, in incredible myriads, gleaming cold and hard against the infinite empty blackness. We had been hurled out of the atmosphere and into interplanetary space!

Austen had struck! The world of the *Krimlu* was no more! The whole Silver Sea had gone off in a great explosion. From our ever-rising craft we could see the desert spread out around the mountain like a vast yellow sea, rimmed on the south by a steely blue line that was the ocean. The white fire dulled, faded, and was gone as quickly as it had flashed up. The crater of the Mountain of the Moon was left a wild black ruin of jagged, scattered masses of smoking stone. Of the Silver Lake, of the red vegetation upon the upland, of brilliant *Astran*, not a trace was left!

The crater was left far behind in the long arching flight of the rocket. The white frozen brilliance of the stars faded out, the untold glories of the solar corona were dimmed, and blue was restored to the midnight sky. We were plunging toward the desert in the direction of Kanowna. I pulled back the lever and used the full force of the rockets to check our meteor-like flight until the fuel was exhausted. A moment afterward we struck the earth.

We climbed out and left the vessel there on the sand. Just as the stars were coming out that night we arrived at the headquarters of a great sheep ranch. People were very much excited over the earthquake. (The shock of the explosion of the Silver Lake had been registered at every seismographic station in the world.)

The rancher and his wife cared for us with great hospitality, if ill-controlled curiosity. After we had had a week of rest, they took us by automobile to Kanowna. There I astounded them by rewarding their generosity with a magnificent emerald—I still had in my pack a half pound or so of jewels that Naro had brought me from *Astran*.

Melvar ever surprised me with her innocent beauty, her grace and poise, with the ease with which she learned to face new situations, and to meet people. I believe that no one ever suspected that she had not had a lifetime of training in the best of society. We were married at Kanowna, and reached Perth a few days later.

THE END

If you've enjoyed this book, you will not want to miss these terrific titles…

ARMCHAIR SCI-FI & HORROR DOUBLE NOVELS, $12.95 each

D-91   **THE TIME TRAP** by Henry Kuttner
THE LUNAR LICHEN by Hal Clement

D-92   **SARGASSO OF LOST STARSHIPS** by Poul Anderson
THE ICE QUEEN by Don Wilcox

D-93   **THE PRINCE OF SPACE** by Jack Williamson
POWER by Harl Vincent

D-94   **PLANET OF NO RETURN** by Howard Browne
THE ANNIHILATOR COMES by Ed Earl Repp

D-95   **THE SINISTER INVASION** by Edmond Hamilton
OPERATION TERROR by Murray Leinster

D-96   **TRANSIENT** by Ward Moore
THE WORLD-MOVER by George O. Smith

D-97   **FORTY DAYS HAS SEPTEMBER** by Milton Lesser
THE DEVIL'S PLANET by David Wright O'Brien

D-98   **THE CYBERENE** by Rog Phillips
BADGE OF INFAMY by Lester del Rey

D-99   **THE JUSTICE OF MARTIN BRAND** by Raymond A. Palmer
BRING BACK MY BRAIN by Dwight V. Swain

D-100   **WIDE-OPEN PLANET** by L. Sprague de Camp
AND THEN THE TOWN TOOK OFF by Richard Wilson

ARMCHAIR SCIENCE FICTION CLASSICS, $12.95 each

C-31   **THE GOLDEN GUARDSMEN**
by S. J. Byrne

C-32   **ONE AGAINST THE MOON**
by Donald A. Wollheim

C-33   **HIDDEN CITY**
by Chester S. Geier

ARMCHAIR SCI-FI & HORROR GEMS SERIES, $12.95 each

G-9   **SCIENCE FICTION GEMS, Vol. Five**
Clifford D. Simak and others

G-10   **HORROR GEMS, Vol. Five**
E. Hoffman Price and others

If you've enjoyed this book, you will not want to miss these terrific titles...

INVASION FROM ANOTHER DIMENSION!

Are there other worlds existing side by side with ours, yet unseen and unsuspected? Here is the incredible tale of three people who went through the ethereal wall that bars the way to this shadowy realm, a realm known as the Borderland. Beyond that they found a strange land and an even stranger race of intelligent beings, and in the ranks of those beings was a fantastic enemy, the likes of which Earth had never faced.

Before long the greatest city in the world faced death and destruction from forces incomprehensible to the minds of men. And for all their military might, mankind seemed helpless to fight back. All they could do was stand and watch as their world was literally torn apart in front of them.

CAST OF CHARACTERS

ROB MANSE
When the ghosts were first seen he knew Earth was in trouble, but jumping into another dimension wasn't what he'd expected.

WILL GRANT
He was the first to go into the Borderland and he knew all the answers—he just didn't have time to answer all the questions.

BEE GRANT
Will Grant's beautiful sister—she was brave, smart, and more than willing to make the plunge from "reality" into "unreality."

ALA
This shadowy being from another dimension was more than willing to help mankind in the battle against her own people.

BRUTAR
He had stumbled into our world from another dimension—and he liked what he saw, liked it so much he wanted to conquer it.

THONE
The mind of this Fourth Dimensional ruler was so powerful he could render his foes crumpled and inert with a simple thought.

EO
A young man from the Fourth Dimension. He professed a friendship to the Earth visitors—but could he be trusted?

INTO THE
FOURTH
DIMENSION

By
RAY CUMMINGS

ARMCHAIR FICTION
PO Box 4369, Medford, Oregon   97501-0168

*For more information about Armchair Books and products, visit our
website at…*

www.armchairfiction.com

Or email us at…

armchairfiction@yahoo.com

CHAPTER ONE
The Ghosts of '46

THE first of the "ghosts" made its appearance in February of 1946. It was seen just after nightfall near the bank of a little stream known as Otter Creek a few miles from Rutland, Vermont. There are willows along the creek bank at this point. Heavy snow was on the ground. A farmer's wife saw the ghost standing beside the trunk of a tree. The evening was rather dark. Clouds obscured the stars and the moon. A shaft of yellow light from the farmhouse windows came out over the snow; but the ghost was in a patch of deep shadow. It seemed to be the figure of a man standing with folded arms, a shoulder against the tree-trunk. It was white and shimmering; it glowed; its outlines were wavy and blurred. The farmer's wife screamed and rushed back into the house.

Up to this point the incident was not unusual. It would have merited no more than the briefest and most local newspaper attention; reported perhaps to some organization interested in psychical research to be filed with countless others of its kind. But when the farmer's wife got back to the house and told her husband what she had seen, the farmer went out and saw it also; and with him, his two grown sons and his daughter. There was no doubt about it, they all saw the apparition still standing motionless exactly where the woman had said.

There was a telephone in the farmhouse. They telephoned their nearest neighbors. The telephone girl got the news. Soon it had spread to the village of Procter, and then to Rutland itself. The ghost did not move. By ten o'clock that evening the road before the fanner's house was crowded with cars; a hundred or more people were trampling the snow of his cornfield cautiously, from a safe distance regarding that white motionless figure.

It chanced that I was also an eyewitness to this, the first of the ghosts of '46. My name is Robert Manse. I was twenty-six years old that winter—correspondent in the New York office of a Latin-American export house. With Wilton Grant and his sister Beatrice—whom I counted the closest of my few real friends—I was in Rutland that Saturday evening. Will was a chemist; some business which he had not detailed to me had called him to Vermont from his home near New York. In spite of the snowy roads he had wanted to drive up and had invited me to go along. We were dining in the Rutland Hotel when people began talking of this ghost out toward Procter.

It was about ten-thirty when we arrived at the farm. Cars were lined along the road in both directions. People trampling the road, the fields, clustering about the farmhouse; talking, shouting to one another.

The field itself was jammed, but down by the willows along the creek there was a segment of snow as yet untrampled, for the crowd had dared approach so far but no farther. Even at this distance we could see the vague white blot of the apparition. Will said, "Come on, let's get down nearer. You want to go, Bee?"

"Yes," she said.

We began elbowing and shoving our way through the crowd. It was snowing again now. It was very dark—but some of the people had flashlights that darted about and occasionally a smoker's match would flare. The crowd was good-natured; with courage bolstered by its numbers, the awe of the supernatural was gone. But they all kept at a safe distance.

Somebody said, "Why don't they shoot at it? It won't move—can't they make it move?"

"It does move—I saw it move, it turned its head. They're going up to it pretty soon—see what it is."

I asked a man, "Has it made any sound?"

"No," he said. "They claim it moaned, but it didn't. The police are there now, I think—and they're going to shoot at it. I don't see what they're afraid of. If they wanted me to I'd walk right up to it." He began elbowing his way back toward the road.

WE FOUND ourselves presently at the front rank, where the people were struggling to keep themselves from being shoved forward by those behind them. Thirty feet across the empty snow was the ghost. It seemed, as they had said, the figure of a man, blurred and quivering as though molded of a heavy white mist at every instant about to dissipate. I stared, intent upon remembering what I was seeing. Yet it was difficult. With a quick look the imagination seemed to picture the tall lean figure of a man with folded arms, meditatively leaning against the tree trunk. But like a faint star, which vanishes when one stares at it, I could not see a single detail. The clothes, the face, the very outlines of the body itself seemed to quiver and elude my sight when I concentrated my attention upon them.

Yet the figure, motionless, was there. Half a thousand people were now watching it. Bee said, "See its shoulder, Rob! It isn't touching the tree—it's inside the tree. It's leaning against something else, inside the tree!"

The dark outline of the tree-trunk was steady reality; it did seem as though that shadowy shoulder was within the tree.

A farmer's boy beside us had a handful of horseshoes. He began throwing them. One of them visibly went through the ghost. Then a man with a star on the lapel of his overcoat fired a shot. It spat yellow flame. Where the bullet went no one could have told, save that it hit the water of the creek. The specter was unchanged.

The crowd was murmuring. A man near us said, "I'll walk up to it. Who wants to go along?"

"I'll go," said Will unexpectedly; but Bee held him back.

The volunteer demanded, "Officer, may I go?"

"I ain't stoppin' you," said the man with the star. He retreated a few steps, waving his weapon.

"Well then put that gun away. It might go off while I'm down there."

Somebody handed the man a broken chunk of plank. He started slowly off. Others cautiously followed behind him. One was waving a broom. A woman shouted shrilly, "That's right—sweep it away—we don't want it here." A laugh went up, but it was a high-pitched, nervous laugh.

The man with the plank continued to advance. He called belligerently, "Get out of there, you! We see you—get away from there!" Then abruptly he leaped forward. His waving plank swept through the ghost; as he lunged, his own body went within its glow. A panic seemed to descend upon him. He whirled, flailing his arms, kicking, striking at the empty air as one tries to fight off the attack of a vicious wasp. Panting, he stumbled backward over his plank, gathered himself and retreated.

The white apparition was unchanged. "It was just like a glow of white light," the attacker told us later. "I could see it—but couldn't feel it. Not a thing—there wasn't anything there!"

The ghost had not moved, though some said that it turned its head a trifle. Then from the crowd came a man with a powerful light. He flooded it on the specter. Its outlines dimmed, but we could still see it. A shout went up. "Turn that light off! It's moving! It's moving away!"

It was moving. Floating or walking? I could not have told. Bee said that distinctly she saw its legs moving as it walked. It seemed to turn; and slowly, hastelessly it retreated. Moving back from us. As though the willows, the creek-bank, the creek itself were not there, it moved backward. The crowd, emboldened, closed in. At the water's edge we stood. The figure apparently was now within or behind the water. It seemed stalking down some invisible slope. Occasionally it turned aside as though to avoid some obstruction. It grew smaller, dimmer by its greater distance from us until it might have been the mere reflection of a star down there in the water of the creek; then it blinked, and vanished.

There were thousands who watched for that ghost the following night, but it did not appear. The affair naturally was the subject of widespread newspaper comment; but when after a few days no one else had seen the ghost, the newspapers began turning from the serious to the jocular angle.

THEN, early in March, the second ghost was reported. In the Eastern Hemisphere this time. It was discovered in midair, near the Boro Badur, in Java. Thousands of people watched it for over an hour that evening. It was the figure of a man, seated on something invisible in the air nearly a hundred feet above the ground. It sat motionless as though contemplating the crowd of watchers beneath it. And then it was joined by other figures! Another man, and a woman. The reports naturally were confused, contradictory. But they agreed in general that the other figures came from the dimness of distance; came walking up some invisible slope until they met the seated figure. Like a soundless motion picture projected into the air, the crowd on the ground saw the three figures in movement; saw them—the reports said—conversing; saw them at last move slowly backward and downward within the solid outlines of the great temple, until finally in the distance they disappeared.

Another apparition was seen in Nome, another in Cape Town. From everywhere they were now reported. Some by daylight, but most at night. By May the newspapers featured nothing else. Psychical research societies sprang into unprecedented prominence and volubility. Learned men of spiritualistic tendencies wrote reams of ponderous essays, which the newspapers eagerly printed.

Amid the reports now, the true from the false became increasingly difficult to distinguish. Notoriety seekers, cranks and quacks of every sort burst into print with weird tales of ghostly manifestations. Hysterical young girls, morbidly seeking publicity, told strange tales which in more sober days no newspaper would have dared to print. And in every country charlatans were doing a thriving business with the trappings of spiritualism.

In late July the thing took another turn. A new era began—a sinister era that showed the necessity for something more than all this aimless talk. Four men were walking one night along a quiet country road near a small English village. They were men of maturity, reputable, sober, middle-aged citizens. Upon the road level they observed the specters of four or five male figures, which instead of remaining motionless rushed forward to the attack. These ghosts were ponderable! The men distinctly felt them; a vague feeling, indescribable, perhaps as though something soft had brushed them. The fight, if such it could be called, amounted to nothing. The men flailed their arms in sudden fear; and the apparitions sped away. Greenish, more solid-looking than those heretofore seen.

This was more than mere visibility—an actual encounter. These four men were of the type who were credible. The report was reliable. And the next night, in a Kansas farmhouse, a farmer and his wife were awakened by the scream of their adolescent daughter. They rushed into her bedroom. She was in bed, and bending over her was the apparition of a man. It s fingers were holding a lock of the girl's long black hair. At the farmer's shout, the ghost turned; its hand was raised—and the farmer and his wife both saw that the shadowy fingers had lifted the girl's tresses that they were clutching. Then it dropped them and moved away, not through the walls of the room, but out through the open window.

The girl was dead. She had suffered from heart trouble; was dead of fright, undoubtedly. It was the beginning of the era of menace. And that next afternoon Wilton Grant telephoned me. His voice had a strange tenseness to it, though it was grave and melodious as always.

"Come out and see us this evening, will you, Rob?"

"Why, yes, I said. I had not seen them for over a month—an estrangement that I had not understood and which hurt me had fallen between us. "Of course I will," I added. "How's Bee?"

"She's been, quite ill... No, not dangerous, she's better now. Don't fail us, Rob. About eight o'clock... That's fine. We—I need you. You've been a mighty good friend, letting us treat you the way we have—"

He hung up. With an ominous sense of danger hanging over me, I went out to see them at the hour he had named.

CHAPTER TWO
Groping at the Unknown

WILTON GRANT was at that time just under forty. He was a tall, spare man of muscular build, lean but not powerful. His smooth-shaven face was large-featured, rough-hewn, with a shock of brown hair above it—hair turning gray at the temples. Beneath heavy brows his gray eyes were deep-set, somber. His ruddy brown complexion, the obvious strength of his frame at a quick glance gave him an out-of-doors look; a woodsman cast in the mould of a gentleman. Yet there was something poetic about him as well—that wavy, unruly hair, the brooding quality of his eyes. When he spoke, those eyes frequently twinkled with the good nature characteristic of him. But in repose, the somberness was there unmistakable—an unvoiced, brooding melancholy.

Yet there was nothing morbid about Wilton Grant. A wholesomeness, mental and physical, radiated from him. He was a jolly companion, a man of intellectuality and culture. His deep voice had a pleasing resonance suggestive of the public speaker. Normally rather silent, chary of speech, he could upon occasion draw fluently from a vocabulary of which many an orator would be proud.

He was a bachelor. I often wondered why, for he seemed of a type that would be immensely attractive to women. He did not avoid them—the pose of a woman-hater would have been abhorrent to him. Yet no woman to my knowledge had ever interested him, even mildly. Except his sister. They were orphans and she was his constant companion. They were both in fact, rather chary of friends; absorbed in their work, in which she took an active part. Their home and laboratory was an unpretentious frame cottage in a Westchester village of suburban New York. They lived quietly, modestly, with only one automobile, and no plane.

Will opened the door for me himself, smiling as he extended his big, hearty hand. "Well! You came, Rob? You're very forgiving—that's the mark of a true friend." He led me into the old-fashioned sitting room. "I'm not going to apologize—"

"Don't," I said. "I knew of course you had some reason—"

We were seated. He said with a nod, "Yes. A reason—you'll hear it now—tonight—"

His voice trailed away. It made my heart beat faster. He had changed. I saw him suddenly older.

"Where's Bee?" I asked out of the silence.

He jerked himself back from his reverie. "Upstairs. She'll be down in a moment. She's been ill, Rob."

"But you said not seriously."

"No. She's better now. It's been largely mental—she's been frightened, Rob. A terrible strain—that's why I thought it better for us to isolate ourselves for a while—"

"Oh, then that's why—"

"That's why I wrote you so peremptorily not to come to see us anymore. I was upset myself, I needn't have been so crude—"

"Please don't apologize, Will. I—I didn't understand, but—"

"I'm not appologizing. I'm just telling you. But now Bee thought we should have you with us. Our best friend, you understand? And it will make things easier for her—naturally she's frightened—"

My hand went to his arm. What I had meant to say I do not know, for Bee at that moment entered the room. A girl of twenty-four. Tall, slim and graceful.

She was dressed now in a clinging negligee, which seemed to accentuate the slim grace of her. But the marks of illness were plain upon her face; a pallor; her eyes, though they smiled at me with the smile of greeting upon her lips, had the light of fear in them; her hand as I took it was chill, and her fingers felt thin and wan.

"Bee..."

"It's good to see you, Rob. Will has been apologizing for us, I suppose—"

These friends of mine calling me to them in their hour of need. I had been annoyed, hurt; I had not realized how deep was my affection for them...for Bee... Vaguely I wondered now if their trouble—this fear that lay so obviously upon them both—concerned the coming of the ghosts.

Bee sat close beside me, as though by my nearness she felt a measure of protection.

WILL faced us. For a moment he was silent. Then he began, "I have a good deal to say, Rob—and I want to be brief—"

I interrupted impulsively, "Just tell me this. Does it—this thing whatever it is—does it concern the ghosts?"

I was aware of a shudder that ran over Bee. Will did not move. "Yes," he said. "It does. And these ghosts have changed. We knew they would—we've been expecting it."

"That poor girl," Bee said softly. "Dead—dead in her bed of fright. You read about it, Rob?"

"A menace," Will went on. "The world is just realizing it now. Ghosts, changing from shadow to substance—" He stopped, then added abruptly, "We've never told you much about our work—our business—have we?"

They had in truth always been reticent. I had never been in their laboratory. They were engaged I understood, chiefly with soil analysis; sometimes people would come out to consult them. Beyond such a meager idea I knew nothing about it.

Will said abruptly, "Our real work we have never told anyone. It concerns—well, a research into realms of chemistry and physics unknown. I have been delving into it for nearly ten years, and then Bee grew old enough to help me. We've made progress—" His smile was very queer. "Tonight—I'm ready to show you something that I can do."

They seemed to torture Bee, these words of her brother's. I heard the sharp intake of her breath, saw her white fingers locked tensely in her lap.

"Not—not tonight, Will."

"Tonight—as good a night as any other. Rob, would it surprise you to know we anticipated the coming of the ghosts years ago? Not that they would come, but the possibility of it. Ghosts! What do you think they are, Rob?"

"Why ghosts—ghosts are—"

"Spirits of the dead made visible?" His manner was suddenly vehement, his tone contemptuous. "Earthbound spirits! Astral bodies housing souls whose human bodies are in their graves! Rubbish! These are not that sort of ghosts."

I stammered, "But then—what are they?"

"Call them ghosts, the word is as good as any other." His voice grew calmer; he went on earnestly, "I want you to understand me—it's necessary—and yet I must not be too technical with you. Let me ask you this—you'll see in a moment that none of this is irrelevant. How many dimensions has a point?"

At my puzzled look he smiled. "I'd better not question you, Rob, but you won't find me hard to understand. A point—an infinitesimal point in space—has no dimension. It has only location. That's clear, isn't it? A line has one dimension-length. A plane surface has length and breadth; a cube, length, breadth and thickness. The world of the cube, Rob, is the world we think we live in—the world of three dimensions. You've heard of that intangible something they call the fourth dimension? We think it does not concern us—but it does. We ourselves have four dimensions. We are the world of the fourth dimension. But the fourth is not so readily understood as the other three."

He paused for an instant, then added, "The fourth dimension is time, Rob. Not a new conception to scientists. Think a moment—how would you define time?"

"Time," I said. "Well, I read somewhere that time is what keeps everything from happening at once..."

HE DID not smile. "Quite so. It is something in the universe of our consciousness along which we progress in measured rate from birth to death—from the beginning to the end.

"We are living in a four-dimensional world—a world of length, breadth, thickness and time. The first three, to our human perception, have always been linked together. Time—I do not know why—seems to our minds something essentially different. Yet it is not. Our universe is a blending of all four.

"Let me give you an example. That book there on the table—it exists because it has length, breadth and thickness. But Rob, it also has duration. It is matter, persisting both in space and in time. You see how the element time is involved? I'll go further. We know that two material bodies cannot occupy the same space at the same time. With three of the dimensions only—that is, if theoretically we remove the identical time factor—they do not conflict. You're confused, Rob?"

"I'm not quite sure what you're aiming at," I said.

"You'll understand in a moment. Matter, as we know it, is merely a question of vibration. Is it not?"

"I know light is vibration," I responded. "And sound. And heat, and—"

He interrupted me. "The very essence of matter is vibration. Do you know of what matter is composed? What is the fundamental substance? Let us see. First, we find matter is composed only of molecules. They are substances, vibrating in space. But of what are molecules composed? Atoms, vibrating in space. Atoms are substance. Of what are they composed?"

"Electrons?" I said dubiously.

"Protons and rings of electrons. Let us cling to substance, Rob. These electrons are merely negative, disembodied electricity—not matter, but mere vibration. They—these electrons—revolve around a central, positive nucleus. This then, is all the substance that matter has. But when you penetrate this inner nucleus, what do you find? Substance? Not at all. This proton, as they sometimes term it, this last inner stronghold of substance, is itself a mere vortex—a whirlpool in space!"

I groped at the thought. Matter, substance, everything tangible in my whole conscious universe, robbed of its entity, reduced to mere vibration in empty space. Vibration of what?

"It's appalling, Rob, the unreality of everything. Metaphysicians say that nothing exists save in the perception of it by our human senses. I was talking of the dimension, time. It is the indispensable factor of vibration. That's obvious. Motion is nothing but the simultaneous change of matter in space and time. You see how blended all the factors are? You cannot deal with one without the others. And mark you this, Rob—you can subdivide matter until it becomes a mere vortex in empty space. Can you wonder then—"

I had noticed Bee gazing intently across the room. "Will!" she said suddenly; her voice was hardly more than a whisper. "It's there now, Will!"

THE room was brightly illuminated by a cluster of globes near the ceiling. Will left his seat, calmly, unhurried, and switched them off. There was only the small table light left.

It cast a yellow circle of light downward; most of the room was in shadow. And over in a corner I saw the glowing apparition of a recumbent man no more than ten feet from us.

Will said, "Come here, Rob—let me show you this." His voice was grave and unflurried. As I crossed the room hesitatingly, Bee was with me, forcing herself to calmness. She said, "It's here most of the time. Watching us! It seems to be on guard—always watching—"

Will drew me beside him and we stood within a foot of the spectre. It took my courage, but after a moment the gruesome element of it all seemed to leave me, for Will stood as though the thing were a museum specimen, explaining it.

I saw, so far as I can put the sight into words, the vibrating white shape of a man reclining on one elbow. It was slightly below the level of the floor, most of it within or behind the floor, the outlines of which were plainer than the apparition mingled with them. The head and shoulders were raised about to the level of our ankles.

A man? I could not call it that. Yet there was a face, which after a moment I could have sworn was human-featured; I thought I could almost see its eyes, staring at me intently.

Will stooped down and passed his hand slowly through the face. "You can feel nothing. It has visibility—that property only in common with us. Try it."

I forced my hand down to the thing, held it there. It was like putting one's fingers into a dim area of light.

"Is it—it is alive?" I asked.

"Alive?" Will's tone was grim. "That depends on what you mean by alive. It can reason, if that answers you."

"I mean—can it move?"

"It moves," said Bee. "It watches us—follows us—" She shuddered.

The details of the figure? I stepped back to see it better. It seemed now a man clothed in normal garments...a malevolent face, with eyes watching me... Was the face my imagination, or did I really see it?

I MUST have stammered my thoughts aloud, for Will said, "What we see, and what really exists, has puzzled metaphysicians for centuries. Who knows what this thing really looks like? You do not, nor do I. Our minds are capable of visualizing things only within the limits of an accustomed mould. You see that thing as a man of fairly human aspect, and so do I. The details are elusive, but stare at them for a day and your imagination will supply them all. That's what you do in infancy with the whole material world about you—mould it to fit our human perceptions. But what everything really looks like—who can tell?"

"Can it—can it hear us?" I demanded.

"No—I do not think so. It can see us, no more. And it has no fear." With a belligerent gesture he added humorously, "Get up, you, or I'll wring your neck!"

"Will, don't joke like that!" Bee protested.

He turned away and switched on the main lights. I could still see the thing there, but now it was paler—wan like starlight before the coming dawn. Will turned his back on it and sat down. His face had gone solemn again.

"These things are materializing, Rob. They have become a menace. That's why what I'm planning to do should be done at once—

"But Will—

"Bee! Will you please not interrupt me!" It was the first time I had ever heard his tone turn sharp with her, and I realized then the strain he was under. "Rob, listen to me. Science has given me the power to do what I'm planning, but we won't discuss that now. Call this anything you like. What

I want you to know is, there is another realm about us into which—under given conditions—our consciousness can penetrate. Call it the "Unknown." The realm of "Unthought Things." A material world? I've shown you, Rob, that nothing is substance if you go to the inside of it."

Dimly I was groping at a hundred will-o'-the-wisps, my mind trembling upon the verge of his meaning, my imagination winging into distant caverns of unthought things that hid in the elusive dark. Could this be science?

He was saying, "My mind cannot fathom such another realm, nor can yours. You think of land, water, trees, houses, people. Those are only words for what we think we see and feel. But there are beings—sentient beings—in this other state of consciousness, we can now be sure. For Rob, they are coming out! Don't you understand? They have already come into the borderland between the consciousness of their realm and ours,"

He would not let me interrupt him. "Let us say they have a lust for adventure—or a lust for something else—they are coming out nevertheless. A menace to us—that girl in Kansas is dead." He swept his hand in gesture at the apparition behind him. "That thing is watching me. As Bee says, it is on guard here. Because, Rob, I found a way of transmuting my identity out of this conscious realm of ours into that same borderland where these things we call ghosts are roaming. And they know it—and so they're on guard—watching me."

He paused for the space of a breath. Bee, white-faced, tremulous, turned to me. "Don't let him do it, Rob!"

"I must," he declared vehemently. "Rob, that's why we needed you here—to wait here with Bee. I'm going in there tonight—into the shadows, the borderland, whatever it is. These nameless things are striving to come out, but I'm going to turn them back if I can..."

CHAPTER THREE
Into the Shadows

THERE were few preparations to make, for Wilton Grant had planned this thing very carefully. Our chief difficulty was with Bee. The girl was quite distraught; illness, the fear that for weeks had been dragging her down, completely submerged the scientist in her. And then abruptly she mastered herself, smiled through her tears.

"That's more like it, Bee." Will glanced aside at me with relief. "I couldn't understand you. Why Bee, we've been working at this thing for years."

"I'm all right now." She smiled at us—a brave smile though her lips were still trembling. "You're—about ready, aren't you?"

They had set aside a small room on the lower floor of the house—a sort of den, which now was stripped of its accustomed hangings and furniture. It had two windows, looking out to the garden and lawn about the house. They were some six feet above the ground. It was a warm mid-summer evening; we had the lower sashes opened, but the shades fully drawn lest some neighbor or passerby observe us from without. On the floor of the room lay a mattress. There was a small table, a clock, two easy chairs. For the rest it was bare. Its white plaster walls, devoid of hangings, gave it somewhat the sanitary look of a room in a hospital.

We had been so occupied with Bee that Will had as yet given me no word of explanation. He left the little room now, returning in a moment with some articles that he deposited on the table. I eyed them silently; a shiver of fear, apprehension, awe—I could not define it—passed over me.

Will had placed on the table a carafe of water; a glass; a small vial containing a number of tiny pellets; a cylindrical object with wires and terminal posts which had the appearance of a crude home-made battery—four wires each some ten feet in length, terminating each in a circular metallic band.

I glanced at Bee. Outwardly now she was quite composed. She smiled at me. "He'll explain in a moment. Rob. It's quite simple."

We were ready. By the clock on the table it was twenty minutes of ten. Will faced us.

"I'd like to start by ten o'clock," he began quietly. "The time-factor will be altered—I want to compute the difference—when I return—as closely as I can."

I had the ill grace to attempt an interruption, but he silenced me.

"Wait, Bob—twenty minutes is not a long time for what I have to say and do." He had motioned us to the easy chairs, and seated himself cross-legged on the mattress before us. His gaze was intent upon my face.

"This is not the moment for any detailed explanation, Rob. I need only say this: As I told you a while ago, the fundamental substance of which our bodies are composed is—not substance, but a mere vortex. A whirlpool, a vibration let me term it. And the quality of this vibration—this vortex—the time-factor controlling it governs the material character of our conscious universe. From birth to death—from the beginning to the end—we and all the substance of our universe move along this unalterable, measured flow of time.

"Do I make my meaning clear? From—nothing but a vibrating whirlpool the magic of chemistry has built with this unalterable time-factor what we are pleased to call substance—material bodies. These material bodies have three varying dimensions—length, breadth and thickness.

But each of them inherently is endowed also with the same basic time-factor. The rate of time-flow governing them, let me say, is identical."

He spoke now more slowly, with measured words as though very carefully to reach my understanding.

"You must conceive clearly, Rob, that every material body in our universe is passing through its existence at the same rate. Now if we take any specific point in time—which is to say any particular instant of time—and place in it two material bodies, those two material bodies must of necessity occupy two separate portions of space. That's obvious isn't it? Two bodies cannot occupy the same space at the same time.

"Now Rob, I have spoken of this unalterable measured flow of time along which all our substance is passing. But it is not unalterable. I have found a way of altering it."

He raised his hand against my murmur, and went on, carefully as before. "What does this do? It gives a different basic vibration to matter. It gives a different rate of time-flow, upon which, building up from a fundamental vortex of changed character, we reach substance—a state of matter— quite different from that upon which our present universe reposes. A different state of matter, Rob—it still has length, breadth and thickness—but a different flow of time.

"You follow me? Now, if we take a material body of this—call it secondary state—and place it in the same space with a body of our primary state, they can and do occupy that space without conflict at the same instant of time.

"Why? Ah Rob, it would take a keener mind than mine or yours to answer that, or to answer the why of almost anything. The knowledge we poor mortals have is infinitesimal compared to the knowledge we have not. I can conceive vaguely however, that two primary bodies, placed in identical points of space and time would be moving through time at identical rates and thus stay together and conflict. Whereas, with a primary and secondary body, their differing time-flows would separate them after what we might call a mere infinitesimal instant of coincidence."

HIS gesture waved away bat part of the subject. He rose to his feet. "I have particularized even more than I intended, Rob. Let me say now, only that the pellets in this little vial contain a chemical, which acts upon the human organism in the way I have described. It alters the fundamental vibration upon which this substance—these bones, this flesh we call a body—this substance of my being, is built.

"Just a moment more, Rob, then you shall question me all you like. So much for the transmutation of organic substance. Inorganic substance—that table, my shirt, that glass of water—theoretically all of them could be transmuted as well. I have not, however, practically been able to accomplish that. But I have—invented, if you like, an inorganic substance that I can transmute. It is nameless; it is this."

He was coatless, and now he stripped off his white linen shirt. Like a bathing suit, he had on a low-cut, tight-fitting garment. It seemed a fabric thin as silk, yet I guessed that it was metallic, or akin to metal. A dull putty-color, but where the light struck it there was a gleam, a glow as of iridescence.

"This substance," he added, "I can—take with me." He indicated the wires, the battery if such it were. "By momentarily charging it, Rob, with the current I have stored here. It is not electrical—though related to it of course—everything is—our very bodies themselves—a mere form of what we call electricity."

He was disrobing; the gleaming garment fitted him from shoulder to thigh. About his waist was a belt with pouches;

in the pouches small objects all of this same putty-colored substance.

I burst out, "This is all very well. But how—how will you get back?"

"The effect will wear off," he answered. "The tendency of all matter, Rob, is to return to its original state. I conceive also that in the case of human organism, the mind—the will—to some extent may control it. Indeed I am not altogether sure but that the mind, properly developed, might control the entire transmutation. Perhaps in this secondary state, it can. I am going to be leaving that to chance, to experimentation."

I said, "How long will you be gone?"

He considered that gravely. "Literally, Rob, there is no answer to that—but I know what you mean, of course. I may undergo a mental experience that will seem a day, a week, a month—measured by our present standards. But to you, sitting here waiting for me—" He shrugged. "By that clock there, an hour perhaps. Or five hours—I hope no more."

My mind was groping with all that he had said. I was confused. There was so much that I no more than vaguely half understood; so much that seemed just beyond the grasp of my comprehension, I seemed to have a thousand questions I would ask, yet scarce could I frame one of them intelligently. I said finally:

"You say you may be gone what will seem a day, yet by our clock here it will be only a few hours. This—this other state of existence then moves through time faster?"

"I conceive it so, yes."

"But then—are you going into the future, Will? Is that what it will be?"

He smiled, but at once was as grave as before. "Your mind is trying to reconcile two conditions irreconcilable. You may take an apple and try to add it to an orange and think you get two apple-oranges. But there is no such thing. Our future—let us call it that which has not yet happened to us but is going to happen. I cannot project myself into that. If I could—if I did—at once would the future be for me no longer the future, but the present.

"The conception is impossible. Or again—in this other state—I must of necessity exist always in the present. Nor can you compare them—reconcile one state of existence with the other." He stopped abruptly, then went on with his slow smile. "Don't you see, Rob, there are no words even, with which I can express what I am trying to make you realize. That being reclined there in the other room a while ago and watched us. Perhaps for what it conceived to be what we would conceive a day were we to experience it."

His smile turned whimsical. "The words become futile. Don't you see that? The future of that being is merely what has not yet happened to it. To compare that with our own consciousness is like trying to add an apple to an orange."

DURING all this Bee had sat watching us, listening to our talk, but had not spoken. And as, an hour before in the other room I had noticed her glancing fearsomely around, again now her gaze drifted away; and I heard her murmur.

"Oh, I hoped it would be gone—not come to us in here!"

We followed her gaze. Standing perhaps a foot lower than the floor of our room and slightly behind the side wall was that self-same spectral figure. The intent to watch us, to enter perhaps into a frustration of our plans, with which my imagination now endowed its purpose, made me read into its attitude a tenseness of line; an alertness, even a guarded wariness which had not seemed inherent to it before. Was this thing indeed aware of our purpose? Was it waiting for Wilton Grant to come into the shadows to meet it upon its own ground? With an equality of contact, was it then planning to set upon him?

Bee was murmuring, "It's waiting for you. Will, it's waiting for you to come—" Shuddering words of apprehension, of which abruptly she seemed ashamed for she checked them, going to the table where she began adjusting the apparatus.

"I'm coming," said Will grimly. "It will do well to wait, for I shall be with it presently." He stood for a moment before the thing, contemplating it silently. Then he turned away, turned his back to it; and a new briskness came to his manner.

"Rob, I'm ready. Bee knows exactly what we are to do. I want you to know also, for upon the actions of you two, in a measure depends my life. I shall sit here on the mattress. Perhaps, if I am more distressed than I anticipate, I shall lie down. Bee will have charge of the current. There will come a point in my departure when you must turn off the current, disconnect the wires from me. If I am able, I will tell you, or sign to you when that point is reached. If not—well then, you must use your own judgment."

"But I—I have no idea—" I stammered. Suddenly I was trembling. The responsibility thrust thus upon me seemed at that moment unbearable.

"Bee has," he interrupted quietly. "In general I should say you must disconnect when I have reached the point where I am…" He halted as though in doubt how to phrase it. "…the point where I am half substance, half shadow."

To my mind came a mental picture, which then seemed very horrible; but resolutely I put it from me.

"You're ready, Bee?" he asked.

"Quite ready, Will." She was counting out a number of the tiny pellets with hands untrembling. The woman in Bee was put aside; she stood there a scientist's assistant—cool, precise, efficient.

"I think I should like less light," he said; and he turned off all the globes but one. It left the room in a flat, dull illumination. He took a last glance around. The window sashes were up, but the shades were lowered. A gentle breeze from outside fluttered one of them a trifle. Across the room the spectre, brighter now, stood immobile. The clock marked one minute of ten.

"Good," said Will. He seated himself cross-legged in the center of the mattress. In an agony of confusion and helplessness I stood watching while Bee attached the four wires to the garment he wore. One on each of his upper arms, and about his thighs where the short trunks ended.

Again I stammered, "Will, is this—is this all you're going to tell us?"

He nodded. "All there is of importance. A little tighter, Bee. That's it—we must have a good contact."

"I mean," I persisted, "when you are—are shadow, will we be able to see you?"

He gestured. "As you can see that thing over there, yes."

His very words seemed unavoidably horrid. Soon he would be—a thing, no more.

"Shall you stay here, Will, where we can see you?"

He answered very soberly, "I don't know. That, and many other things, I don't know. I will do my best to meet what comes."

"But you'll come back here—here to this room, I mean?"

"Yes—that is my intention. You are to wait here, in those chairs. One of you always awake, you understand—for I will need you, in the coming back."

THERE seemed nothing else I could ask, and at last the moment had come. Bee handed him the pellets, and held the glass of water. For one brief instant I had the sense that he hesitated, as though here upon the brink the human fear that lies inherent to every mortal must have rushed forth to stay his hand. But an instant only, for calmly he placed the pellets in his mouth and washed them down with the water.

"Now—the current, Bee."

His voice had not changed; but a moment after I saw him steady himself against the mattress with his hands; momentarily his eyes closed as though with a rush of giddiness, but then they opened and he smiled at me while anxiously I bent over him.

"All right—Rob." He seemed breathless. "I think—I shall lie down." He stretched himself at full length on his back, and with a surge of apprehension I knelt beside him. I saw Bee throw on the little switch. She stood beside the table, and her hand remained upon the switch. Her face was pale, but impassive of expression. Her gaze was on her brother and I think I have never seen such in alert steadiness as marked it.

A moment passed. The current was on, but I remarked unmistakably that no sound came from it. The room indeed had fallen into an oppressive hush. The flapping shades momentarily had stilled. Only the clock gave sound, like the hurried thumping of some giant heart, itself of all in the room most alive.

Wilton Grant lay quiet. His eyes were fixed on the ceiling; he had gone a trifle pale and moisture was on his forehead, but his breathing, though faster, was unlabored.

I could not keep silent. "You all right, Will?"

At once his gaze swung to me. A smile to reassure me plucked at his parted lips. "All right, yes." His voice a half-whisper, not stressed, almost normal; and yet it seemed to me then that a thinness had come to it.

Another moment. The putty-colored garment he wore had lost the vague sheen of its reflected light and was glowing with an illumination now inherent to it. A silver glow, bright like polished metal; then with a greenish cast as though phosphorescent. And then, did I fancy that its light, not upon it or within it, but behind it, showed the garment turning translucent?

I became aware now of a vague humming. An infinitely tiny sound—a throbbing hum fast as the wings of a humming bird, near at hand, very clear, yet infinitely tiny. The battery—the current; and yet in a moment with a leaping of my heart. I knew it was not the current but a humming vibration from the body of Wilton Grant. A sense of fear—I have no memory adequately to name it—swept me. I rose hastily to my feet; as though to put a greater distance between us I moved backward, came upon a leather easy chair, sank into it, staring affrighted, fascinated at the body recumbent before me.

THE change was upon it. A glow had come to the ruddy pink flesh of the arms and legs, bared chest, throat and face. The pink was fading, replaced, not by the white pallor of bloodlessness but by a glow of silver. A mere sheen at first, but it grew into a dissolving glow seeming progressively to substitute light for the solidity of human flesh.

And then I gasped. My breath stopped. For behind that glowing, impassive face I saw the solid outlines of the mattress taking form, saw the mattress through the face, the chest, the body lying upon it.

Wilton's eyes were closed. They opened now, and his arm and hand with a wraith-like quality come upon them, were raised to a gesture. The signal. I would have stammered so to Bee, but already she had marked it and shut the current off.   And very quietly, unhurried, she bent over and disconnected the wires, casting them aside.

The humming continued; so faint, so rapid I might have fancied it was a weakness within my own ears. And presently it ceased.

Bee sat in the chair beside me. The body on the mattress was more than translucent now; transparent so that all the little tufts of the mattress covering upon which it lay were more solidly visible than anything of the shadowy figure lying there. A shadow now; abruptly to my thought it was Wilton Grant no longer.

And then it moved. No single part of it; as a whole it sank gently downward, through the mattress, the floor, until a foot or so beneath, it came to rest. With realization my gaze turned across the room. The silent spectre was still there, standing beneath the floor, standing I realized, upon the same lower level where the shadow of Wilton Grant now was resting.

I turned back, saw Bee sitting beside me with white face staring at the mattress; and I heard myself murmur. "Is he all right do you think? He hasn't moved. Shouldn't he move? It's over now, isn't it?"

She did not answer. And then this wraith of Will did move. It seemed slowly to sit up; and then it was upright, wavering. I stared. Could I see the face of my friend? Could I mark this for the shadow of his familiar figure, garbed in that woven suit? It seemed so. And yet I think now that I was merely picturing my memory of him; for surely this thing wavering then before me was as formless, as indefinable, as elusive of detail as that other, hostile spectre across the room.

Hostile! It stood there, and then it too was moving. It seemed to sweep sidewise, then backward. Ah, backward! A thought came to me that perhaps now fear lay upon it. Backward, floating, walking or running I could not have told.

But backward, beyond the walls, the house, smaller into the dimness of distance.

Was the shadow of Wilton Grant following it? I could not have said so. But it too was now beyond the room. Moving away, growing smaller, dimmer until at last I realized that I no longer saw it.

We were alone, Bee and I, alone to wait. The mattress at my feel was empty. I heard a sound. I turned. In the leather chair beside me Bee was sobbing softly to herself.

CHAPTER FOUR
The Return

THE hours seemed very long A singular desire for silence had fallen upon us. For myself, and it is my thought that the same emotion lay upon Bee, there were a myriad questions upon which idly I would have spoken. Yet of themselves so horrible, so fearsome seemed their import that to voice them would have been frightening beyond endurance.

Thus, we did not speak; save that at first I comforted Bee, clumsily as best I could, until at last she was calmer, smiling at me bravely, suggesting perhaps that I would sleep while she remained on watch.

The clock ticked off its measured passing of the minutes. An hour. Then midnight. The window shade was flapping again with the night wind outside. I rose to close the sash, but Bee checked me.

"He might want to come in that way. You understand, Rob—"

Memory came to me of the half-materialized spectre of that Kansas farmhouse, that apparition so ponderable of substance that it must perforce escape by the opened window. I turned back to my chair.

"Of course, Bee. I'd forgotten,"

We spoke in hushed tones, as though unseen presences not to be disturbed were around us. Another hour. Throughout it all with half closed eyes I lay back at physical ease in my chair, regarding the white walls of our little room so empty. We still kept the single dull light; dull, but it was enough to illuminate the solid floor, that starkly empty mattress, the white ceiling, the four walls, closed door at my side, the two windows, one of gently flapping shade. And as musingly I stared the sense of how constricted was my vision grew upon me. I could see a few feet to one blank wall or another, or to the ceiling above, the floor below, but no further. Yet awhile ago, following the retreat of those white apparitions, my sight had penetrated beyond the narrow confines of this room into distances illimitable. And to me then came a vague conception of the vast mystery that lay unseen about us, unseen until peopled by things visible to which our sight might cling.

The realm of unthought things! Yet now I was struggling to think them. The realm of things unseen. Yet I had seen of them some little part. The wonder came to me then, were not perchance, unthought things non-existent until some mind had thought them, thus to bring them into being?

Two o'clock. Then three. Five hours. He had said he might return in five hours. I stirred in my chair, and at once Bee moved to regard me.

"He will be coming, soon," I said softly. "It is five hours, Bee."

"Yes, he will be coming soon," she answered.

Coming soon! Again I strove with tired eyes to strain my vision through those solid walls. He would be coming soon; I would see him, far in the distance, which his very presence would open up to me.

And then I saw him! Straight before us. Beyond the wall, with unfathomable distances of emptiness around him. It might have been our light gleaming upon an unnoticed protuberance of the rough plaster of the wall, so small was it; hilt it was not, for it moved, grew larger, probably coming toward us.

Bee saw it. "He's there! See him, Rob!" Relief in her tone, so full to make it almost tearful; but apprehension as well, for to her as to me came the knowledge that it might not be him.

Breathless we watched; waited; and the white luminosity came forward. Larger, taking form until we both could swear it was the figure of a man. Lower now, beneath the level of our floor. It came, stopped before us almost within the confines of the room.

We were on our feet. Was it Wilton Grant? Was this his tall, spare figure—this luminous, elusive white shape at which I gaped? Did I see his shaggy hair? Was that his brief woven garment? I prayed that my imagination might not be tricking me.

Bee's agonized call rang out. "Will! Is this you, Will?"

WE STOOD together; she clung to me. The figure advanced, stood now quite within our walls. No longer wholly spectral, a cast of green had come to it—a first faint semblance of solidity. It stood motionless—drooping, as though tired and spent. Was it Wilton Grant? It moved again. It advanced and sank into the floor as though sitting down—sitting almost in the center of the mattress, though a foot beneath it. Significant posture! It had come to the mattress it had departed from. It was Wilton Grant!

We bent down. Bee was on her knees. Now we could see details, clearly now beyond all possibility of error. Will's drawn face, haggard, with the luminosity every moment fading from it, the lines of opaque human flesh progressively taking form.

He was sitting upright, his hands bracing him against that unseen level below us. Then one of his hands came up, queerly as though he were dragging it, and rested on the higher level of the mattress. His eyes, still strangely luminous, were imploring us. And then his voice, a gasp; and a tone thin as air.

"Raise—me! Lift—me up!"

Bee's cry was a horror of self-reproach, and I knew then that she must have neglected the instructions he had given her. We touched him; gripped him gently. Beneath my fingers his half-ponderable flesh seemed to melt so that I scarce dared press against it. We raised him. There was little weight to resist us; but as we held him, the weight grew. Progressively more rapidly; and within my fingers I could feel solidity coming.

Again he gasped, and now in a voice of human labored accents. "Put me—down. Now—try it, Bee."

We lowered him. The mattress held him. At once he sank back to full length, exhausted, distressed—but uninjured. Bee gave him a restorative to drink. He took it gratefully; and now, quite of human aspect once more, he lay quiet, resting.

Bee's arms went down to him.

"Will, you must go to sleep now—then you can tell us—"

"Sleep!" He sat up so abruptly it was startling. More strength had already come to him than I had realized. "Sleep!" He mocked the word; his gaze with feverish intensity alternated between us.

"Bee—Rob, we've not time right now for a long three-sided conversation. I'm all right—quite recovered. But you must listen to me, both of you. What I have been through— seen, felt—you could never understand unless you experienced it. No time for talk—I must go back!"

A wildness had come to him, but I could see that he was wholly rational for all that; a wildness, born of the ordeal through which he had passed.

"I must go back, at once. The danger impending to our world here—is real—far worse than we had feared. Impending momentarily—I had feared it—but now I know. And I must go back. With you—I want you two with me. You'll go, Bee, Rob, will you go?

A sudden calmness had fallen upon Bee. "I'll go of course," she said quietly.

"Yes, of course. And you, Rob? Will you go with us? We need you."

Would I go? Into the unnamable, the shadows of unthought, unseen realms, to encounter—what? A rush of human fear surged over me; a trembling; a revulsion; a desire to escape, to ward off the horror that crowded toward me. Would I go? I heard my own voice say strangely:

"Why—why yes, Will, I'll go."

Go! Leave this world!

And my voice was telling them calmly that I would go!

CHAPTER FIVE
Last Preparations

COMMITTED thus by my own quiet words, involuntarily spoken as though by a volition apart from me, I strove for calmness. A confusion of mind possessed me. But Bee was quite calm; and presently, though within me the surge of apprehension continued, outwardly I believed I did not show it.

Three of us going into the shadows. And Will said not to linger this time in the Borderland, but to go on—to penetrate into the depths of the Unknown realm beyond. The wry thought of it brought a score of anxious questions to my mind; but when I tried to voice them Will crisply checked me.

I realized now, with an emotion tinged by a faint whimsicality, that Will and Bee had summoned me here this evening with an anticipation of just this outcome. They had foreseen that we all three would make the trip together. They were prepared for it; and Will's first trial had been experimental wholly.

Thus, I found them ready. Two others of the knitted suits were at hand. Two other batteries. But we—Bee and I—had been seemingly indispensable in aiding Will. His departure—Bee had been by his side to remove the buttery wires. And far more important, when it returned, his solidifying shadow had lain beneath the mattress. We had been there to raise him up, to hold him until the substance of his body was great enough for the mattress to sustain it. Suppose we had not raised him? Suppose while yet within the mattress space—or within the space the floor of the room itself was occupying—the growing solidity of him had demanded empty space of its own? The thought brought a shudder—a thought too horrible to be dwelt upon.

During our brief preparations—which Will hurried with a grim taste—he did not once volunteer to explain his experience. And only once did Bee question him.

"You'll tell us exactly what we are to do?"

"Yes. Presently—before we start."

"You said there was need of haste? A real danger to our world here—from those—other beings?"

He was arranging the batteries. "Yes, Bee. A real danger."

"You think we can repulse them? Just three of us going in there? Strangers—"

Strangers indeed. No adventurers into other lands in all the dim pages of history could have felt, or been, such strangers.

He interrupted her. "We will do our best. It is necessary—our efforts... We will have plenty of time for consultation, Bee. You will understand, when we are there... Pour three glasses of water, Rob."

My fingers were trembling; it seemed strange that Bee could contain such calmness. But it was simulated for she said:

"Will, is it—is it very horrible—the changing, I mean?"

He stopped before her, put his hands on her shoulders. His face, so set with its purpose he had forgotten the human feelings of her, softened momentarily with affection.

"No—it is strange—frightening at first. But not horrible. And you forget it soon. Then it's merely strange, awesome— you'll see—"

He broke off, turned away, and as momentarily his gaze touched me, he smiled. "Awesome, Rob. But for me, this second time, it will be no great ordeal. Even exhilarating— strangely so. You'll see... We're about ready, Bee."

She took her woven suit and retired. I was soon undressed and into mine. Its fabric was queerly light of weight, and for all its metallic quality it stretched readily, almost like rubber as I put it on. Somehow donning that garment made me shudder. It seemed unnaturally chill as it touched my skin.

Bee presently returned, garbed as we were. In spite of my perturbation and my fear of the dread experience that lay before me, I felt a thrill of admiration as I beheld her. So slim of figure, straight of limb, graceful; and with her grave, intelligent face full of one set purpose—to aid us in every way she could.

"We're ready," said Will briefly. "Here are your belts."

We fastened the broad belts about our waists. The pouches each contained some small object.

"Don't bother them now," Will objected, as I would have examined them. "Later, when we get in there, will be time enough... We're ready. What we are to do now is simple—I think there will be no mishap. We will seat ourselves on the mattress. You two may lie down; I shall sit up this time."

"Why?" I demanded.

HE SMILED. "It is only the first time one feels the sensations that they are disturbing. I'm confident of that. We will have the batteries beside us—" Bee was already placing them on the mattress. "At my signal, we will each disconnect our own. Should either of you be unable—be overcome—I will do it for you."

"But the coming back," I suggested, "we raised you up—"

His smile held a faint ironic amusement. "Don't you think we can leave that to its proper time?" He saw my look and added, with the ready apology that made him so lovable:

"Naturally you are apprehensive. But I've planned for that, of course. There are many places where the level of this Borderland—as I call it—coincides exactly with the surface of our own realm. The back corner of the garden outside, for instance. I have marked it—I can find it—when the time comes for us to return."

Bee said, "Will, I've been wondering—you were gone five or six hours. Were you in there very long?"

His smile was enigmatic. "You can have no conception of this experience. I can't answer. That's why I haven't told you anything. You are so soon to feel and see it for yourself." He was impatient for the start. "I think we're ready. There is so little to do—no chance to forget anything."

With sudden irrelevant thought my heart leaped. That hostile watching spectre... My anxious glance traveled the room. Bee said, "It's not here—I've been expecting—I'm so thankful it's not here."

It wasn't to be seen. I was relieved for that, at least. With a last deliberation we seated ourselves on the mattress. Will was between Bee and me. We connected the batteries; I held mine at my side, my nerve-shaken fingers trembling, though inwardly I cursed them, fumbled at the switch to make sure I could control it. The pellets were in the palm of my other hand; the glass of water was within reach.

Will said earnestly, "One last thing—and this is important—more important than you realize. Whatever comes, we must keep together. Remember that. You two—strive always to keep with me—close beside me. Whatever impulse you feel—fight it—do not yield to it. Remember you must stay by me."

The words themselves were simple to grasp. Yet beneath them lay a vague import, a suggestion of what was to come, which seemed unutterably sinister. I heard Bee murmuring.

"Yes, I understand."

I said, and marveled at the steadiness of my voice. "Very well, Will—I'll remember."

He said, "Now." I saw his hand go to his mouth. Now I must take the pellets. Within me a torrent of revulsion surged. I must take the pellets—at once. Bee was raising her glass of water. My hand went up; I felt the pellets in my mouth. Acrid. A faint acrid taste spread on my tongue. And then with a gulp of the water I had swallowed them. Breathless I waited, with heart thumping like a hammer, my head reeling, not from the pellets but from the excitement and fright that swept over me uncontrolled.

Will's voice said. "Rob. Your battery—switch it on."

My fingers found the little switch, pushed it. I felt a faint tingling of my limbs; a sudden nausea possessed me; my senses whirled; the room, which all at once had grown very sharp of outline, turned nearly black.

CHAPTER SIX
The Mind Set Free

I DID not faint, and in a moment I felt better. My vision cleared; the room regained almost its normal aspect. But the nausea persisted. I felt a desire to lie down. Will was sitting erect, but beyond him I saw Bee lying on her side, facing us. I reclined on one elbow, holding up my head that I might look around me.

The faintness was gone. The sweat of weakness was upon me, my forehead cold and clammy; but I could feel my heart beating strongly. When was the change to start? It seemed ages since I had taken those pellets.

Then I heard the hum. It sounded as though apart from me; but I knew it was not for I could feel it. A vibration. Not of my knitted suit; a vibration within me; within the very marrow of my bones.

My gaze was fixed upon the table across the room. Its outlines were very sharp and clear, unnaturally so, with that sharpness of detail which sometimes comes to the vision of one who is ill. Now they began to blur—an unsteadiness as though I were looking through waves of heat. Had the change started? I raised my hand, examined it. No change, save that the receding blood had made it a little pale.

The nausea was now leaving me. A sense of relief, of triumph that I was not ill possessed me. With every alert faculty I determined to remark my sensations.

The vibration within me grew stronger, though to my ears it was unaltered. And then, abruptly the change began. My whole being was quivering. Not my muscles, my flesh, my nerves, but the very matter that composed them suddenly made sensible to my consciousness. The essence of me, trembling, quivering, vibrating—a tiny force, rapid beyond conception. It swept me with a tingling, grew stronger, possessed me until for a moment nothing of my consciousness remained but the knowledge of it.

Frightening, horrible—but the horror passed. Again my brain and vision cleared. My whole being was humming; and then I realized that I could no longer hear the hum, merely felt it. The knowledge of sound not the sound itself. And an exhilaration was coming to me. A sense of lightness. My body growing lighter, less ponderable. But it was far more than that. An exhilaration of spirit, as though from me shackles of which I was newly conscious, were melting away. A lightness of being. A freedom... A new sense of freedom, frightening with the vague wild triumph it brought. Frightening too, for in the background of my mind was the realization that all my physical perceptions were dulling. My elbow was resting sharp against the rough mattress. I dragged my arm a trifle; and dull, far away as though detached from me, I could faintly feel it. I moved my leg. It was not numb. The reverse, it was thrilling in its every fibre. It moved, but I could only feel it move as in a dream. I even wondered if I felt it move at all. Was it not, perhaps, only my *knowledge* that it moved?

Abruptly I became aware that the table across the room had changed. My mental faculties, with all this morbid change of the physical taking place about them, were still alert. I had vaguely expected the table, the room, the visible, material objects of the realm I was leaving, to remain unaltered of aspect. But they did not. The table had lost its color; a monochrome of grayness possessed it. The table, the chairs, the whole room, had turned flat and gray. Flat of tone and flat of dimensions well. The flat printed picture of a room.

But in a moment even that had changed. The gray outlines of the table were dim and blurred; the gray substance of it, no longer dull and opaque, seemed growing luminous, faintly phosphorescent. Translucent, then transparent. Through the table leg, through the wavering gray image of the room-wall, I saw opening up to me the vast darkness of an abyss of distance. A phantom room in which I lay. The shadow of a room hovering in empty space.

THERE was no horror within me now. That thrilling sense of lightness, that vague unreasoning triumph of loosened shackles had no thought of horror; and to me came a faint contempt for this phantom room, these imponderable shadows which once had been solid chairs and walls.

Then I heard Will's voice. "The battery! Turn off your current, Rob!"

Heard his voice? I believe I barely heard it—physically a thin wraith of human voice striking my eardrums. Yet, mingled with that realization, was the sense that he was speaking quite normally. With my mind's ear, the *memory* of his normal voice made me hear his hurried, anxious admonition. "Turn off your battery, Rob!"

My battery. Of course, the moment had arrived when I must turn it off. I glanced down at it. A shadowy, unreal, phantom battery lying beside me; my gray hand resting upon it seemed to my vision far more ponderable. And then I received my first real perception as to the nature of this change. My fingers groped for the switch, found it. But this shadow battery, of which even then I was dimly contemptuous, was solid beyond all solidity of which I had ever formed conception. My fingers fumbling with it— dulled, as were my physical sensations. I could feel those fingers groping as though the adamant steel of that switch was *penetrating them*. A feeling indescribable—uncanny, morbidly horrible, though the incident was so brief the horror scarce had time to reach my confused consciousness. My fingers, not the battery, were shadow—half ponderable fingers, feeling their way *within the solid steel* of that tiny switch. For a terrifying instant I thought I could not move it. Then—it moved; the current was off. I sank back, exhausted of spirit with the effort. But at once Will's voice aroused me.

"Disconnect the wires. Can you do it, Rob? Quickly—or it will be too late."

I fumbled for the wires; cast them off—gigantic cables they might have been to the futile wraiths of my ringers. Will helped me, I think; and at last I was free, lying back upon the mattress. Dimly I could feel it beneath me, my thrilling, vibrating body resting upon it as though I were a feather newly drifted down.

Moments passed. I do not know how long. I could not have told for my thoughts were winging away unfettered, untrammeled as in a dream...a dream...the past, the present—all of it savored of a vaguely pleasant reality.

And presently I realized that I was moving; my body— could I indeed call this vanished consciousness of the physical a body?—my being was floating, drifting gently downward, I could no longer feel the mattress; I saw it—a blurred, gray, transparent shadow, coming upward. Beside me, *within me;* then over me as I sank through it a foot or two and came to rest.

Beneath me now, there was a dull sensation. I could feel myself lying upon something apparently solid. Feel it? The feeling was barely physical; rather was it a mere knowledge that I was lying there.

I tried to keep my scattering thoughts together. It was an effort to hold them—an effort to think coherently; an effort to cling to anything—even mental—of reality. I told myself that the change must be nearly complete. *I* was the spectre;

this phantom mattress, this wraith of a room—those ghost-like chairs and table floating in space above me—that was my own real world, lost and gone.

A silence had fallen. The hum within me no longer sounded. It was a shock to see that little phantom clock; the movement of its pendulum was visible, but its ticking heart gave no sound. A preternatural silence hung like a gray shroud over a universe of shadows. Then I heard Will's *soundless voice*—heard it clearly now with the knowledge that it was wholly mental, a transference of thought, which only my imagination and memory endowed with a familiar physical timbre.

"Rob. Come back to us! Hold your thoughts. Stay here with us."

And Bee's imploring voice, "We are here, Rob. All here together. Sit up—look at us—speak to us."

Was I indeed, nothing now but a mind? Were my thoughts all that remained of me? I fought for reality, for stability; fought for anything real that I could clutch, to which desperately I might cling. Where were Will and Bee? Somewhere here in the shadows. An abyss of shadows everywhere. I thought I could see a thousand miles into that pregnant darkness. I could wander in it at will; my thoughts could wander everywhere.

But I must have conquered, for I found myself sitting up, with Bee and Will beside me.

"THERE, that's better." I felt the relief in Will's lone. "Hold yourself firm—you'll be used to it in a moment. It's strange, isn't it?"

Strange, scarce have I words—and even those I choose are almost futile—to picture what I saw and felt. The world I had left lay all about me—dim, transparent shadows of familiar things. The room of Will's house—we were sitting just below the level of its floor. Around the room—above it, to one side of it—the phantom house itself was visible. Beyond the house, the gardens, the somber ghosts of trees standing about—a shadowy semblance of the winding village street—other houses—a hill in the distance—

Mingled with all these shadows, the reality I had left was the reality in which now I existed. The Borderland, we had been calling it. A vast realm of luminous darkness. A rolling slope upon which we were sitting—a slope, something newly tangible at least, which I could vaguely see and vaguely feel beneath me. A realm of pregnant darkness, tilled with the shadows of the world I had left; and filled also with things as yet unseen-things as yet unthought... The realm of unthought things...

Will's voice seemed saying, "So strange—but you'll be used to it presently."

I turned to regard him and Bee—these spectres like myself, sitting beside me. What did I see? What was their aspect to this new mind's eye that was mine? I cannot say. I think now that my intelligence saw the intelligence that was theirs, and clothed it out of habit with a semblance of substance for a body—familiar of outline and form since there was no other aspect I could conceive. I saw—or thought I saw, which perhaps is quite the same—luminous gray ghosts of my companions as last I had seen them. Of themselves they appeared not transparent. Through them the spectral walls of the room were not visible; of everything around me the bodies of my friends seemed the most real.

Will was smiling at me reassuringly. Bee's gaze was affectionate. Their voices, save that I knew I heard no sound, seemed not abnormal. I spoke. It was like thinking words with moving lips. But they heard me; not to read my lips, but to hear my thoughts. Heard with a result quite normal, for they nodded and smiled and answered me.

THEN Will touched me; experimentally with a smile, he laid his hand upon my arm. It was not unreal, save that only dimly, as though my senses were dulled, could I feel him. Yet there was a *weight* to his grip. His tenuous ghostly fingers (as I would have counted them in my former state) were not ghostly of grip to me now. His fingers, my arm, were identical of substance. His fingers could not occupy the space with me; they were ponderable, real, with a dulled reality that gave me at last something to cling to; brought my scattering thoughts together. I was here—Robert Manse— alive, living, breathing, sitting beside my friends. From that moment a measure of the strangeness left me and took to itself the externals only. *I* was real; Bee and Will were real; it was only the things around us which were strange. The body, which momentarily I seemed to have lost, was restored to me. A sense of the physical; dulled of perception, but still a body to house my mind. To house it—yet not to hold it firmly. A body which now was not a prison; shackles fallen away, yet there was a danger to that. Already I had tasted of it—for the mind, too free, is difficult to control.

I was saying, "I'm—all right... I was dreaming—I got confused."

Bee said whimsically, "We're here. Will, there is so much I want to ask you—"

"Not now, Bee." His voice was full of its old decisiveness. "We must start. Keep together—you understand now Rob, what I meant. Keep together—keep thinking, firmly, what you are doing. And do—what I do. We must start."

He drew himself erect. As though I were dreaming—or thinking of the act—I felt myself standing erect. Then walking—vaguely I could feel the substance of the slope beneath my feet—walking with a lightness, a lack of effort weird but pleasant. And I clung physically to Will, and saw

Bee on his other side clinging to him also—as though a breath of wind might blow us all away.

The thought was whimsical. There could be no wind. Wind was moving air. I had the sense that I was still breathing, of course. But how could there be air? Air itself was infinitely more solid than these, our bodies. Yet I was breathing something. Call it air. The word of itself means nothing—and there are no words with which to clothe the realities of any unthought realm...

We were walking through the phantom room which had been the reality of Will's home—through its wall—out through its garden. Our slope was rolling, uneven. The shadowy ground of the garden was above us, then below us; then for a moment, we seemed standing exactly on its level. I remembered. This was the place Will had mentioned to which we could safely return.

We spoke seldom; Will did not seem to care to talk. I realized it knew where he was going—had some definite purpose in his mind. Alert now with every mental faculty, I wondered what it was, yet would not question him.

We stalked onward. The shadowy village lay about us, above us now. Soundless, colorless phantoms, these streets, trees and houses. I saw the railway station—the ghost of a train stood off there and then moved forward soundlessly. I was touched with a faint amusement to see it—a luminous ghost sliding along its narrow enslaving rails. It could not go up or down, or sidewise, and it seemed so imponderable I would fearlessly have walked into it.

This Borderland, full of these shadows of our other world, yet seemed empty. Nothing of its own reality was visible. In every direction I could look into seemingly infinite distance; and overhead was a vast darkness—the emptiness of infinite space. Was nothing here with us in this Borderland? Those other spectres—those beings coming out from their world as we were coming in from ours...?

A thrill of quite normal excitement swept me at the thought. We had come in to encounter those spectres. And now they would be spectres no longer. Ponderable beings upon an equality with ourselves; and we were here to thwart them of their purpose...

I heard Bee give a faint, alarmed cry. Ahead of us a shape had appeared! It became visible and I felt that perhaps it had been hiding behind some unseen obstacle. It stood, solid and gray, with the shadow of a barn, a haystack above and behind it. Stood directly in our path, as though waiting for us.

I pulled at Will, but he ignored me. Hastened his pace.

We stalked forward with that waiting thing—standing immobile in our path!

CHAPTER SEVEN
The Struggle at the Borderland

THE thing stood waiting as Will drew us toward it. Fear swept over me. Yet the very sense of fear brought with it a reassurance, for it was the physical I feared; the vanished sense of my body was not entirely gone, for now I was fearing its welfare.

My voice protested. "Will, wait. That thing there—"

"It is friendly, Rob."

The fear died. I remembered what now seemed obvious; Will had been leading us somewhere with a set purpose. To meet this friendly thing, of course; this thing which doubtless he had met before. I stared at it as we approached. A dim, opaque gray shape like ourselves; but it seemed formless, sexless; neither human nor unhuman—a shape merely—a some thing poised there of which my mind seemed able to form no conception. Then I heard Will say to Bee:

"A girl. Bee—you understand—Rob, listen. We must cling to the realities of our world. There are no other words—no other conceptions—with which we can think these unthought things. This is a girl—"

I thought it was a girl and at once I fancied that I could distinguish her. Standing there with a phantom barn and haystack of our own world above and behind her. A girl like Bee. I could see the gray-formed outlines of her; vaguely flowing draperies; long hair; a face of human beauty with a queer wistful look—she was smiling at Will—a friendly smile—

All this I thought I saw; and in the thinking, brought it to reality. Into my mind then flashed a clearer understanding. This Borderland—and the other inner realm lying beyond it that soon we were to enter—could no more be compared to the world we had left than an apple can be added to an orange. The very essence of every thought we now were thinking was different—incomparable. Yet within our minds was some lingering, unchangeable quality—call it Ego—so that these new things must be clothed in the fashion of the old.

My words grow futile? I can only say then that this first encountered being seemed like a girl, wistful of face; gray, colorless of aspect; yet solid—as solid as ourselves which every moment was seeming a more normal solidity.

Will touched her. "Rob—Bee—this is Ala—she has been waiting for us."

Her voice said, "I am Ala who will do what I can to help you."

The tone seemed soft, liquid, musical and wholly feminine. Soundless words but clearly intoned as though I had heard them with a physical ear.

Bee said, "Why she speaks English."

It struck a note of whimsicality; the thought momentarily relieved the tension under which I was laboring. And so I think it was with the others; they were smiling; but Will's smile faded as he turned to us.

"You must keep on thinking things like that. Cling always to normality." His voice was earnest. "You also, Ala— English you see, is our language."

"But you are speaking my language," she said gravely.

"Of course," he agreed hurriedly.

"Do not doubt it. All of you—I think I understand best of us all. We must strive for our accustomed normality. Remember—the mind now is nearly everything."

"I am—not really confused," I said.

It relieved him; he spoke more quietly. "This girl, Ala, came from her own realm—wandered out here to see and feel for herself what madness was possessing her people."

"IT IS strange," Ala said abruptly. "I am frightened—" Sudden terror marked her features. I was standing nearest to her and her hand gripped me. Again I felt that solidity. Normality. I was real; I laughed contemptuously at all these shadows. The girl added anxiously:

"Can't we go back? Now—where all is real—not like this. I can't stay here much longer."

"We will go," said Will. "Bee—and you Rob—listen carefully. From now on it is a question of the power of our minds—our will power. If you wander—weaken for a moment—we are lost. Keep thinking 'I am here with my friends. We are going together—going into the other realm.'" He swung to the girl. "You, Ala, for you it is easier. But yield yourself slowly. If you withdraw resistance you will rush beyond us. You understand? Above everything else we must keep together."

She nodded.

We clung to each other. Ala began moving forward, drawing us onward up that empty Borderland slope which now was steeply inclined. We passed through the haystack—a mere shadow; passed upward through a corner of the barn roof.

Beneath us now spread the phantom world we had left. But as my thoughts dwelt on what we were going to do, the shadows of our earthly realm seemed fading, growing dimmer, blurring as though about to vanish. I watched them fearfully. When they were gone I would be in darkness—pregnant darkness thronged with things unseeable. I thought vehemently.

"We must keep together—we are going on into that other realm. Will says we are. Will says we must keep together."

But my thought strayed. I remembered Will's house; the room we had left—the little clock. Why, I fancied I almost saw it. Was I there, back in that room? Where was Bee? Bee...?

I must have called her name in my thoughts, and at once she answered.

"Here, Rob, here." And I felt the pressure of her hand.

A struggle of the mind. I knew then that every quality of mind inherent to me was winging backward: tugging, pulling, but I fought against it. And I became aware too of a different struggle within me. I had sensed it for some time past but now it sprang into keen intensity. A struggle of the physical. A vague racking pain possessed me—dull, detached seemingly from my consciousness—yet I knew it was the pain of my body. It grew sharper. Not intolerable, but frightening with a sense of horror. It permeated my every fiber; tingling with infinitely tiny needles; and tugging, physically as my mind was tugging, to resume its original state. Like a chip in an undertow I was being drawn backward...

"Now." I felt Will's tense voice. And Ala's soft words. "We—are—passed. Hold me—now."

Someone was clutching my arm. I seemed floating, storm-tossed—a feather blown in a wind I could not feel. But abruptly the struggle ceased; vaguely I was conscious that my feet were standing upon something solid—Will and Bee were here—Ala was here—I was a reality once more, and there were rational thoughts to think and real things to see.

CHAPTER EIGHT
The Realm of New Dimensions

THE shadows of our world were vanished. The Borderland, with its darkness, its drab empty slope, was gone. A new world lay spread about me, new companions. And I was conscious of a new entity—a new Robert Manse, who was myself.

I remember now that my first thought was surprise that I should be able to visualize things of strangeness. But now I know that once over the Borderland my mind itself had changed, yet retaining of its old self just enough, so that I might be conscious of the strangeness. In a gray half-light of luminosity seemingly inherent to everything, I found myself standing upon a hillside, gazing down an empty slope of grayness. Was it land? I can only say that it seemed solid beneath me; solid, quivering with a tiny tremble; vibrating, and within itself vaguely luminous.

Overhead was darkness. Yet hardly that, for the same luminosity was there; and I felt that I was gazing, not through emptiness but rather through some tenuous fluid illimitable to my vision, with things there to see, as yet—for me—unseeable.

The slope before me was empty. But shapes were materializing; it was as though I had come out of the darkness, with eyes not yet accustomed to the light. I fancied I saw water in the distance. A white lake; but when I stared, it seemed more like a gray rolling cloud. Was it liquid...?

The mind receives a multitude of impressions in an instant. I was conscious of myself. My body was an entity wholly vague—yet there seemed a tingling in it; a *weight* to it, for I was standing upright. Will and Bee—and the girl Ala— were beside me. I saw them now in their old familiar form, but with a queer sense of *flatness* to them. Flat; unnatural of outline; not grotesque, merely strange, unreal. Almost indescribable; and though distinctly it was not a two-dimensional aspect, I think that *flatness* best describes it. A something about them which was lacking, or perhaps a something added—I do not know.

And inherent to this realm as soon I was to see it, was this same queer flatness. Things without *depth;* yet to view them sidewise, the depth was there, with the flatness still persisting.

And I saw color; nameless colors, which I might call blue, or red, or green and the words would have no meaning. Men, women—houses, or at least habitations; the words are all I can command, but they are grotesquely meaningless. It was all so incomparably strange; and paradoxically the strangest of it all was the fashion in which my mind began to accept it. I could think of Ala as nothing but a girl. A frightened, likable girl—with thoughts and feelings similar to my own. This realm was real—a new country with friends, enemies—a struggle going on within it in which I must play a part. The overall whole seen and thought of in terms of my own world. And I realized that I—to these others of this other realm— must have seemed a stranger, but not so very strange. Thought of by them in their own terms—each of us upon a common ground, an equality of material state, to visualize the other in terms of ourselves.

CHAPTER NINE
The Attack on the Meeting House

ALA was saying, "At last—it is so good to be back." For her the struggle was wholly past; she was smiling, relieved, and upon her face there was solicitude for us. "You are not injured? At rest—now?"

"Yes," said Will, "it's over." His hand touched Bee affectionately. "The strangeness will soon be gone, I think. You all right, Rob?"

"Yes," I said. In truth, every moment a rationality of being was coming to me. And curiosity, of itself evidence of normality, made me ask, "Where are we going? What are we going to do?"

"Going with Ala," said Will briefly. "Her people are friendly to us—deploring the threatened invasion of our world."

I realized that he and Ala at their first meeting must have exchanged knowledge, and planned what we now were to do.

Bee asked, "Are we going far? Will it take long?"

Ala seemed puzzled. "Far? Long?" The words involved Space and Time. I saw that at first they had no meaning to her.

"We are going there," she answered. Her gesture was vaguely downward ahead of us. "Come," she added.

We started. My impression now is that we were walking. I could feel a part of my body in movement, quite as though of my volition I were moving my legs. A sense of lightness again possessed me, a lack of stability. But I could feel solidity beneath me, and I was moving upon it.

We walked then, down the hill. There was vegetation; things, let me say, seemed rooted within the ground, but they bent from our advance as though with a knowledge and a fear that we might tread upon them.

The scene was no longer empty. A rolling land, with what might have been a mountain range rising in the distance. All in that half-light of seeming phosphorescence. I noticed now that the familiar convexity of Earth was gone. The scene had a queer concavity; to the limit of my vision it stretched upward; as though we were upon the inner surface of some vast hollow globe with the concave darkness overhead coming down to meet it. A hollow globe within which we were standing; but it seemed of infinite size.

Not far away now was the region that I first thought was water. We passed over it—partly through it. I felt the resistance against me. Like water with no wetness, but to my sight it was a heavy fog lying upon the land. Its breath was oppressive; I was glad when we were past it, emerging again into the twilight with a city before us.

A city! Houses—human habitations! I knew it—divined it with a new mental alertness; and Ala's words presently confirmed my thoughts.

"Our Big-City," she said.

BEFORE US lay an area upon which was spread a confusion of globes. Circular, yet visually flat of depth. In size I found them later to be, from the smallest some twice my own height, to others I would in my own world have said to be a hundred feet in diameter. Opaque gray globes, of a material unnamable. Of every size they lay seemingly strewn about; and in places piled one upon the other. All of gray color that glistened with a sheen of iridescence.

The Big-City. Diminished by distance it seemed indeed as though a thousand varying-sized soap bubbles, smoke-filled, lay piled together. And the whole flattened, queerly unnatural like a picture with a wrong perspective.

The globes were scattered about; but as we approached I saw open spaces twisting among them like tortuous streets. Horizontal streets, and vertical streets as well. Abruptly I realized that this realm was not cast like my own upon a single plane. On Earth we move chiefly in a world of two dimensions—only in the air or water do we have the freedom of three. Here, the vertical and the horizontal seemed no different.

Bee said, "The Big-City. Houses—" Her voice trailed away into wonderment. From our presently nearer viewpoint movement showed in the city—beings, people like ourselves, moving about the streets. And soon we were among the globes—within the city.

I say "soon." I can remember no conception of time, save in terms of the events within my ken. How *long* it was from our crossing the borderline until we reached the city I do not know—we moved, walked, and entered the city. How far we walked—that too I do not know.

The people we passed did not heed us; the globes, from whatever angle we viewed them, were circular, seemingly flat, but always flat in the unseen dimension. We passed close to one. It appeared solid. It had no apertures—no doors nor windows. A man went by us—a shape in the guise of a man; and he entered the globe by passing through it. It yielded to his passage; its substance closed after him, opaque, sleek, glistening as before.

We stopped at a globe of larger size. Ala said, "I will leave you here. And when I come back—we will go together to the meeting place. They are waiting for you."

Will nodded. "Very well, Ala. How long before you come?"

Again she was puzzled. "How long? Why, I will come."

She left us; I did not see how or where she went.

Will said, "Come on. This is our house—they have given it to us."

Together we passed through the side of the globe. I felt almost nothing—as though I had brushed against something, no more. Were the globes of a material solidity? I do not know.

Within the globe was a hollow interior. Call it a room. The same luminous twilight illumined it. A room of circular concavity. No walls, no ceiling; it was all floor. We walked upon it and though we had passed through it, nevertheless it sustained us; and in every position beneath us seemed the floor, above us the ceiling. A memory of the vanished gravity of our Earth came to me. The word—the conception—had no meaning here. Yet we had *weight;* the substance upon which we rested attracted us perhaps. I cannot say.

We gazed around us. There were places of rest— rectangles of a misty white into one of which I found myself instinctively reclining as though with a need of physical quiet. A sense of ease came to me; but it was only vaguely of the physical. I was indeed now barely conscious of a body, but of my mind I was increasingly aware. I could be tired in mind. I was, and I was resting.

WILL and Bee were resting also. I saw upon Bee's face that same queer, wistful expression that had marked Ala's; I saw her regarding me intently; and I answered her affectionate smile.

Will said, "The strangeness is leaving us. I'm tired—I wish I did not have to talk, but I feel that I should."

He told us then what he had leaned from Ala. This Big-City was the most populous place of the realm. Ala's parent—I might say her father, to make the term more specific—was leader of the Big-City people. One among them—one whom they called Brutar—had found a way to get into the Borderland. He had gone there—and I think that it was he whom we termed the first of the ghosts—whom we had seen that night on the little Vermont farm. He had returned, with tales of an outer world...tales of the consciousness of a different body...a physical being with pleasures unimagined...

The craze to follow him spread. An element undesirable among the people seemed most inspired to join him.

"Ala told me little more than that," Will went on. "The method they are using to get to the Borderland—I do not yet know. But I know that this Brutar—he would sweep with his followers into our world. Physically possessed, in a fashion they could not understand..."

He stopped with the sentence unfinished; it left me with a memory of that Kansas farmhouse, and of the young girl who had died of fright.

Bee asked, "What do they call themselves—these people? This race—beings—" She floundered. "There are no words, yet I have so much to ask."

He shook his head. "All that we have to learn. There is a civilization here—a mental existence in which we'll soon be taking a rational part. For myself, it is less strange every moment."

I nodded. "And Ala's people—they refuse to join in this invasion of our world?"

"Yes," he said. "They deplore it—they're trying to stop it. A meeting is to be held—Ala is coming to take us to it."

I drifted off into a reverie, and Ala came. I glanced up to see her beside us.

"If you are ready," she said, "we will go."

Again we passed through the enveloping globe that was our new home, passed along the city street. It was now deserted. We walked on its level surface; it wound and twisted its way between the globes. At times a group of them piled one upon the other—the smallest on top like a disarray of bubbles—obstructed the street. But the substance upon which we walked (it was often barely visible) turned upward; a sharp upward curve to the vertical; then straight up, again leveling off, and then downward. We trod it, with no more effort going up than upon the horizontal. It seemed, indeed, only as though the scene about us had shifted its plane.

In silence we proceeded. I wondered where the inhabitants of the place might be. Then I saw a few, seemingly not walking openly. One I saw lurking in the curve between two adjacent globes. A man...robed darkly...a dark hood seemingly over his head...like a shroud enveloping him to mingle his outline with the darkness... Darkness? Had the twilight turned to night? Was this the Borderland again? I seemed to see its darkness... I strained my vision for the familiar shadows of our own world... Was that a tree...? A street...? Was that Will's house over there...?

Bee's agonized voice reached my consciousness. "Rob! Rob dear, come back to us!"

My mind had wandered, and had drawn with it the tenuous wraith of a body it so easily dominated. I fought myself back. Told myself vehemently I was *not* in the Borderland; I was with my friends. With Will—Bee, with Ala.

I SAW them, distantly; with Space I know not how much, nor Time, how long—between us. Saw them; saw Bee with horrified arms held out as though to bring me back. And felt myself whirling in Nothingness.

"Rob! Rob!"

"Yes," I called. "I'm here—coming." And at last again I was with them.

"You're careless, Rob." Concern mingled with the relief in Will's tone. "Careless—you must not wander that way."

Ala said quietly. "There are many like that. A wandering mind brings evil to the body it tosses about."

"But with us now, it is additionally hard," Will said. "Every instinct within us draws us away—as it was with you, Ala, in the Borderland."

"Yes," she agreed. "I know that."

We continued our passage toward the meetinghouse. That shrouded shape I had seen was not of my wandering fancy, for now I saw others. Peering at us from dark spaces; eyes that glowed unblinking; or shapes of mantled black skulking furtively along the streets. Avoiding us, yet always watching as we boldly passed.

"Brutars," Ala said. "Those who are with Brutar and would attack your world. They are everywhere now about the city. I am afraid of them."

We came upon the meetinghouse.

It was a tremendous globe, in outward aspect no different from the others save that its size was gigantic. As we neared it I saw that upon its luminous gray surface were narrow circular bands of a lighter color—bands both vertical and horizontal. These also I had noticed on most of the other globes; a lighter color in bands, or sometimes in small patches. I questioned Ala. The lighter-colored parts were where one might safely enter, thus not to encounter the occupants, or the furnishings within.

We passed through one of the bands of the gigantic globe, and found ourselves in a single great room—a globular amphitheater. To use earthly measurements it had perhaps a thousand feet of interior diameter. Its entire inner surface was thronged with gray-white shapes of people, save where, like aisles, the space of the outer bands divided them into segments.

The segments were jammed; the people seemed crouching upon low pedestals, one close against the other. A few of the pedestals were vacant. There were none where we entered, and the nearest I saw were almost above us. We passed along an aisle to reach them. The globe and everyone in it appeared slowly turning over, so that always we seemed to be at its bottom with those opposite to us over our heads.

At last we were seated. In the center of the globe, suspended there in space by what means I could not know, was a ball some fifty feet in diameter. Upon it men were sitting—dignitaries, leaders of the people facing from every angle the waiting throng. And one—a man of great stature, Ala's father—was walking around the ball restlessly, awaiting the moment when he would begin his address.

A silence hung over everything. Again I was reminded of the utter soundlessness of this realm. I felt the suppressed murmurs of the people—but I know no physical sounds were audible. Nor indeed had I eardrums with which to hear them, had such sounds existed.

Time passed as we found our seats. Immobile we sat, and for me at least, time ceased to exist.

Then Ala's father spoke. "My people—danger has come to a strange race of friendly neighboring beings. And it brings a danger also to us all—to you, to me—"

He stopped abruptly. I felt a sound, a myriad of sounds everywhere about us. There were shouts of menace and a swishing, queerly aerial sound as of many rapidly moving bodies.

Through all aisles of the globe, from outside, the shapes of men were bursting. Swishing through the opaque surface of the globe, entering among us, whirling inward. Like storm tossed feathers they whirled, end over end, uncontrolled with the power of their rush. A cloud of hostile gray shapes in the fashion of menacing men came to attack us!

CHAPTER TEN
Captured By Thoughts Malevolent

AS THE followers of Brutar burst into the globular amphitheater with shouts of menace, a confusion, a chaos, a panic descended upon the gathering. Everywhere the people were rising to flight, struggling to escape, struggling with each other—aimlessly, unreasonably, with scarce the steady thought to distinguish friend from foe. The stools upon which we had been sitting were overturned; the floor around me and above me was gray with its surging occupants. They were floating inward, struggling groups of them; the air soon was full of them, like feathers tossed in a breeze. I could feel the breeze now—a turgid motion of that imponderable, invisible fluid for which I have no other name save air; a breeze caused by the fluttering things that were ourselves.

It seemed—as the idea came to me from some dim recess of that other mind that had been mine—it seemed an aimless struggle. I was clutched by a dozen groping hands—pressed by half as many bodies. I saw them—indistinguishable as they rocked against me; and felt them dimly. I fought back, clutched at emptiness; I caught something solid. Pushed it violently away, to see it float off, and feel myself drift backward from the recoil of my blow, the physical futilely struggling with its own tangibility.

A whirling gray shape, definitely outlined in the fashion of a burly man, bore down upon me. It halted, gathered its poise and confronted me. A length away, with empty space between us, it stood motionless. Brutar! Recognition came to me; and I knew then that this was the shape they had termed the first of the ghosts—that spectre we had seen on the bank of the little creek in Vermont. Brutar—he who was leader of these invaders we had come to check. The desire shot through me to attack him now—to kill him.

I plunged; but as though I had leaped into some unseen, entangling veil I was halted; pushed backward until again I found myself facing him. He had not moved. With folded arms he stood regarding me. I stared into his eyes. They were glowing, smoldering torches. A wave of something almost tangible was coming from them; and abruptly I knew that it was his thoughts in a wave so ponderable I could not force my body against it. I could feel it, this wave; feel these thoughts, malevolent, commanding, compelling, as they beat against me.

He spoke. "You need not try to move. You cannot, except as I would have you move."

The words seemed inherent to all the space about me; it was almost as though the words themselves were ponderable; but it was the thought of them—his thought of them—which like a net had me entangled. I struggled, if not to advance, then to retreat. I could do neither. The wave had coiled about me. Matter of a tangibility almost equal to that of my own body, it held me enmeshed. Yielding as I fought with it, but holding me as a delicate net will hold a struggling fish.

He spoke again. "Be still—both of you."

Both of us! I became aware that Bee was beside me, floundering, swept inward toward me, to grip me at last and cling.

"Bee! Bee, dear."

"Rob! It's you! I'm so glad. I tried—I can't get away. I'm entangled—it's all around me. Both of us—we can't get away."

I had no coherent thought remaining, save relief that Bee was with me. I tried to think that I must escape—must kill this Brutar. Like an echo, as though I had shouted them aloud, the thoughts rebounded to beat against my brain with a pain almost physical. I could not think them again. A wall was around me reflecting them back—distorted, agonized echoes, impotent to pass the barrier. And I thought, "I must kill—I—I am glad Bee is with me. Everything is all right— Bee is with me." And yielded, to stand there helplessly clinging to her.

Around us—beyond Brutar's entangling engulfing whirl of thought—I perceived a dim vision of struggling shapes and confused sound. Far away, very far away, far away in distance—in Space, and in Time as well. Why of course— that struggle in the meeting house was in the Past. We were there no longer, either in Space or Time—that struggle in the meeting house had been, but it was not now.

Bee was still clinging to me. Like submerged swimmers sucked away in an undertow, we swirled within that enveloping thought-wave. Brutar was near us. I could see him—see the gray hovering shape of him. Darkness was everywhere. Solidity gone, save the press of those hostile thoughts and the blessed tangibility of Bee within the hollow of my protecting arm.

A chaos of moving darkness. Or was it that the darkness was immobile and ourselves rushing through it? A chaos of things that I could not see; thoughts that I tried to think, but could not. Thoughts rushing past me; entities invisible, uncapturable.

For what length of Time or Space I do not know, Bee and I whirled onward through that dark mental chaos— imprisoned, with our captor leading us.

CHAPTER ELEVEN
The Universe of Thought

I SHALL revert now to Will's experience during that attack upon the meetinghouse as he later described it to me. He had been crouching near Ala. When the hostile shapes burst in, he clung to her. Will was more alert than I to the conditions of this strange existence. He gave no thought to a physical violence; he knew it was the mental struggle that was to be feared; and he kept his mind alert, aggressive to attack.

Ala too, was of help. He heard her murmuring, "Be very careful. Let no evil thought-waves engulf us."

A shape whirled up—a leering man. But Will's thoughts were stronger. The waves clashed with a visible front of conflict; a faint glow of luminous black, in a very palpable heat. The shape cowered, retreated, slunk away.

Everywhere the struggle was proceeding. Upon the center ball Ala's father stood, and with roaring voice and a will more defiant than any within the globe, he strove to quell the invaders. Beat them back. Some retreated; some fell, lying crumpled and inert. Dead? We may call them so. Bodies unharmed. Minds driven into darkness, driven away to leave an empty shell behind them. Soon the confusion was over. The amphitheater was strewn with mindless bodies; the dead—never to move again, and others, injured; minds un-hinged—irrationally wandering, to return, some of them, to reach again their accustomed abode.

Ala's father—they called him Thone—found his daughter with Will and took him to his home, where for a nameless time they were together, exchanging friendly thoughts that each might know what manner of world was his friend's. To

Will it was the first rationality of this new realm. They reclined within a globe of luxurious fittings that gave a sense of peace, luxury, well being of the mind, derived by what means Will could not say. He only was aware that Ala was beside him, her father facing them.

He had thought of Bee and of me with fear—had wondered where we were, had wished we were with him. But Thone had told him not to be afraid. It was so easy to wander. We had not come to harm within the meetinghouse. We would presently come back, or if we did not, he would send out and find us.

The interior of the globe was vaguely luminous. Thone said, "We would perhaps be more comfortable if we could see outside." He murmured words—commands spoken aloud; and a shell of the globe in a patch above them slowly seemed to dissolve—or at least become transparent, so that they saw through it a vista of the city of globes—a city lying then in the vertical plane with the black void of darkness to one side.

THONE was a grave man of dominant aspect; eyes from which shone a power of mind unmistakable. He listened silently while Will tried to describe our Earthly existence. Occasionally he would question, smiling his doubts. At last he said, "It seems very queer to have the mind so enchained by its body."

Then Thone spoke of his own realm. "We Egos—" The word struck upon Will's consciousness with an aptness startling. Egos! Why, of course. These were not people. He—himself—was no longer a man; an Ego, little more.

"We Egos live so different a life. It is nearly all mental. This body—" He struck himself. "It is negligible."

Soon they were plunged into scientific discussion, for only by an attempt at comparison in terms of science could Will hope to grasp the elements of this new material universe. He said so, frankly; and Thone at once acquiesced.

"I will try," he smiled, "to tell you the essence of all we know of—shall we call it the construction of this universe of ours? All we know. My friend, it is only the wise man who knows how little is his knowledge.

"Our world then is a void of Space and Time. The Space of itself is Nothingness, illimitable. Yet to our consciousness it has a shape, a curvature, like this that is around us now." He indicated the hollow interior of the globe. "To traverse it in a single direction, one always tends to return."

Will said: "A globular void of Space. I can understand that. But how big is it?"

"There is no answer to such a question," Thone replied gravely. "To our material existence, our consciousness, it is a finite area, yet within it some of us may go further than others. A mind unhinged takes its body very far—or so we believe—and yet sometimes returns safely. A mind departed from its physical shell, which it then leaves behind—is gone forever. Yet that too, is illogical, for traversing a curved path such as ours—however slight may be the curve—one must eventually return. And out of this we have built a theory that such a mind—or as we call it, an Ego-untrammeled—will return sometime to take a new body. But I must not confuse you with mere theories when there is so much of fact which is confusing enough no doubt."

"That's not confusing," said Will. "We likewise have such a theory—we call it reincarnation."

Thone went on: "We have then, a void of curved Space. Within it exist Thoughts, material entities persisting in Space for a length of Time. Thus Time is brought into our Universe; but not Time as you have described it to me. Ours, like yours, is the measure of distance between two or more events. But the distance is very dimly perceived by our senses."

"Wait," said Will. "Before you discuss Time, let me understand the other. All your material entities are Thoughts? That is incomprehensible to me."

Thone deliberated. "I suppose that is natural," he declared at last. "Your substance—as it appears to you—has a greater solidity than the substance of your mentality."

IT WAS Will's turn to smile. "The latter, with us, has no substance at all. The human mind—as distinct from our physical brain—is wholly intangible. And it is one of the things we know least about."

"Perhaps that is why it seems so unsubstantial," Thone retorted. "At all events, with us mind—qualities are the basic substance out of which all matter is built. A variety of qualities, which vary the resultant product, be it an Ego, or a thing inert, all are from the same source—a thought."

A Universe built from a Thought! Yet to Will then came the realization that our realm is of an essence equally unsubstantial—our own matter—rod, metal, living organisms, what are they of their essence save a mere vortex, a whirlpool of Nothingness?

A question came to Will; and even as he asked it, he knew its answer. "Your Universe built from a Thought? Whose thought? You start with nothing, yet you presuppose the existence of a Mind to think that thought."

"A Mind all-knowing," Thone answered very slowly. "A mind Omniscient. Have you not spoken of your own belief in such a mind? We call it our Creator-Mind—as quite literally it is."

Will said, "Of itself; that is not concrete to me who am in a measure of scientific reasoning."

Thone said warmly, "That is where you of your Earth—as you call it—are wholly mistaken. And indeed, I begin to see where there is not so much difference between your world and mine as we suppose. Let us assume we have the same Creator, his thought to bring us and all that we call our Universe into being."

"Granted," said Will. "But there the similarity ends. You start with a Thought? We start—"

"With what?" Thone demanded.

"Scientifically speaking," Will answered lamely, "we have no beginning. At least, we have not yet been able to explain it."

"We then are more logical than you," Ala put in with a gentle smile.

"Perhaps," agreed Will. "But you cannot connect your Thought with your Science—or at least you have not, to me as yet."

"But I will," declared Thone. "We take this Thought and find it to be a vibration of Nothingness. Of what is your basic substance composed?"

"The same," said Will.

"Quite naturally. We are then of a similar origin—constructed only to a different result. Our substance, in its final state, remains to our consciousness a vibration of Thought. It is quite tangible. Let me show you. Touch me—your hand feels me? That is the physical—cohesive Thought—matter, persisting in Space and Time throughout my existence. Distinct from that, there is my material—mentality. It also persists in Space and Time, but to a lesser degree. More transitory. More varied in its outward qualities, since I can fling out thought-vibrations of good or ill—or many kinds and types.

"Understand me, my friend. This is matter of temporary duration, which I can create myself at will. Or—in terms of your own realm, if you prefer—I can set into vibration, into motion, intangible matter already existing, and by its very motion bring it to tangibility. Can you understand that?"

"YES," agreed Will readily. "And you surprise me with constant similarities to my own world. We believe our own thoughts to be vibrations of some substance intangible. And when you speak of creating an appearance of substance by imparting motion to something otherwise unsubstantial, that too we see in our world. Water is a fluid. A stream of water slowly flowing from a pipe offers no solidity to a blow from a rod of iron. But if that water comes from the pipe with a swift enough motion, a blow struck against the jet with an iron bar seems to be repulsed.

"That seems not actually the creation of new matter, but we have another effect which is this: A tiny rod of steel—a needle the length of my finger—may hang motionless balanced upon a pivot. It is a material body which we would call three or four inches long, by one-hundredth of an inch thick and broad. We set it swinging—vibrating—whirling in a circle with the pivoted end as the center. With a swift enough movement that circle is impenetrable. In effect, out of that needle, we have created a steel disc, one-hundredth of an inch thick, with a diameter of say eight inches. An area of material substance hundreds of times greater than the needle—yet the mass is not increased."

"Quite so," Thone agreed. "Our thought-waves have a mass infinitesimal. But like your steel disc, they can momentarily become very tangible to our Ego-senses. A tangibility very different, yet comparable to our bodies themselves. Less mass, yet more power. Under some circumstances they may alter an inert substance, as I have made transparent to our vision that segment of the globe over there, beyond which we see the city. Or they can enmesh a material organism—your body, for instance—I had meant to demonstrate that."

He moved away from Will, stood quiet; and about Will he flung his wave of thoughts, so that Will was drawn irresistibly to him—as Bee and I were even then enmeshed by Brutar's thought-substance.

Thone laughed. The net of his thoughts dissolved. "You see? It is a very tangible substance. Yet elusive as well. We understand partially its uses. Yet only partially. Its nature is varied from a tenuosity impalpable, to the physical substances that form the entities of our universe. Like that thing you described as your Light-waves, our Thought—substance can traverse Space with tremendous velocity. Not a finite, measurable velocity, as with your Light, but with a speed infinitely rapid.

"A thought may travel to infinity and back in an instant. That—understand me—relates only to its most tenuous form, impalpable to our physical senses—perceived only dimly and only occasionally by a mind other than that from which it originates. In more solid forms its velocity is slower. But it is all under control of our Ego-will power. Do I confuse you?"

"A little," Will admitted. "I am trying to hold a clear conception of it all; I understand you have a void of Space. Must it not be filled with something besides these Thought-entities? Some all-pervading, impalpable fluid?"

"WE DO not know," said Thone frankly. "There are emanations from our immobile organisms. Thus we breathe and eat—the substance of our bodies is renewed—but of that I shall tell you more at another time. You were saying—"

Will went on: "This realm then is filled with your material bodies. This globe we are in—the globes that make your city—the Ego that is you—and myself—other Egos like us.

What holds us where we are?" He smiled. "I'm groping. I'm trying to say, is there no gravitation? No gigantic material body holding us where we are? Out there in the open—" He gestured. "We walked upon something. A surface—a slope. What is it?"

"You ask me many questions at once," Thone replied quietly. "Gravitation, as you call it—yes, with us it is the inherent desire of every particle of thought-matter to cling to its fellows. Thus everything of substantiality tends to cluster at the center of the void. Only motion enables it to depart, which is why it must always move in a curved path—a balancing of the two conflicting forces.

"You question me about some gigantic material substance—like your Earth. There is none. You asked me upon what you walked out there in the open. You walked upon the curvature of Space. Upon a false, a mere semblance of solidity which was the resultant balance of the forces moving you. This globe—this city—it lies immobile upon a solidity equally false—immobile because there is nothing to move it."

"I think I understand a little better," Will said slowly. "All force then, as well as all matter, has its source in the Ego-mind."

"Of course. We create matter, and movement of matter, by our own volition. We have been originally created by the Divine-thought; after which we construct and maintain our Universe by Ego-thought of our own. Inert substance—the mind laboriously creates it; flings it out, solidifies it, moulds it to our diverse purposes. Living organisms—the reproduction of the Ego-species—is similarly of our Ego-mind origin. Yet there is a difference there. For me to reproduce myself in Ala, the Divine-Thought—the assistance shall I say of the Great-Creator—again is necessary. We have not been quite able to fathom why it is so—but it is. There is a difference between an Ego and a thing inert—a vital something which only the Great-Creator can supply."

Ala suddenly interrupted; and upon her face I saw fear. "Your friends—those whom you called Bee and Rob—they are in danger. She—that girl as you called her—that girl Bee—is sending out thoughts of danger. I can feel it."

Thone said: "Try, Ala—could you find her? Where has she gone?"

"I don't know. Her thought-matter is streaming back here. I can feel it—very faintly—but it has reached here. She is with Rob—and there is Brutar."

Thone was upright, with Will beside him. Will was surging with fear. "Danger to them? To my sister—to Rob—"

Thone said: "He has entrapped them—Brutar has entrapped them—all unwary since they do not know how to use these new minds, which are themselves. We must by and get them. Oh, my friend, there is so much that I would tell you—but another time—not now. For if they are in danger we must go to them. That Brutar is a Mind very powerful—"

And out there in the void, Bee and I were being rushed onward. The shape of Brutar with his leering, triumphant face swept ever before us. A dark confusion of mental chaos plunged past. Dismembered, leprous shapes of things, which I thought I saw.

Was this insanity? I felt that evil engulfing net around us—pressing us—dragging us through the darkness.

Then abruptly the scene clarified. The darkness melted before a luminosity so blessed I could have cried aloud with the relief of it. The leprous shapes were gone. Motion stopped; we were at rest, with the net of Brutar's thoughts dissolving from us. Rationality. Again I could think things that were not diseased.

I murmured: "We're all right, Bee. You—you are well again?"

"Yes. Oh, yes, Rob. But I'm so frightened."

Brutar stood before us. "I need you—I am fortunate to have you here. You whom they call Rob—with your knowledge of that Earth-place you can be of great help to me."

He swung toward Bee. "You whom they call a girl—" His twisted look was horrible. "I am glad to have you. We shall go to your Earth together—I welcome you both to this place where we are preparing for our great Earthly conquest."

He led us down a slope, into the strange activities of his encampment.

CHAPTER TWELVE
The Encampment in the Void

BRUTAR said, "Let us go in here. I want to talk to you." We entered a globe very much like those of the Big-City. And reclined at physical ease. But there was no mental peace here—for us at any rate. A turgid aura of restlessness seemed pervading everything.

Brutar rested before us. He seemed always to be regarding Bee; contemplatively, yet with a satisfied triumph.

"I am glad to have you with us," he said, not harshly now, rather with an ingratiating note as though he sought our good will. "We are going to your Earth—to live there, and they tell me, these good people of mine, that they are going to make me its ruler."

He spoke with a false modesty, as though to impress us with his greatness forced upon him by his adoring followers. "I want you two for my friends—you will be of great help to me."

"How?" I demanded. I had recovered from my confusion. I was wary; the thought came to me that I might be able to trick this Brutar. Being here with him and to see and feel what he was doing was an advantage that later on I could turn to account. I wondered if he could hear or feel that thought. I willed it otherwise; and it seemed that he could not. His eyes were upon me, gauging me.

"How could we help you?" I repeated. "And why should we? You mean harm to our world."

"No," he protested. "No harm. We have selected it— your Earth—from all that great Universe of yours that I have inspected. We want to go to your Earth to live. That is all. You can help me, because you know so many things of Earth that I do not. I want you to tell me of them... Stand up!"

I found myself upright, whether by my own volition or his I cannot say.

"Stand up, Bee!"

At his command she also stood erect. He came to us; his hands went to the belts we wore about our waists. I had forgotten my belt—those things in its pouches that Will had bade me not touch. Brutar took them now—my weapons perhaps. And those that Bee carried—took them, discarded them behind him. They floated away; I could barely see them—small formless blobs to my uncomprehending thoughts.

I had very nearly resisted Brutar; but it seemed a futile thing, and I stood quiet. Again we reclined. "Tell me of your Earth," he said; and began to question me.

I told him what I could. I had determined that my best plan was to appear friendly. I wondered how one would escape from a place like this. I was more accustomed to this strange state of being now; knowledge that seemed instinctive was growing within me. I knew that if Brutar's net of thoughts were not to hold me—if I could momentarily be freed of other thought-matter—then I could project myself out into the void. I believed I could find my way back to the

Big-City—once having been there I would have the power to return.

This latter knowledge brought with it a thrill of triumph. I believed that Will and Thone had never been here in Brutar's stronghold. Perhaps this was a secret place that they could not find. But now I had been here; and if I could escape, I could lead others back to it.

With these guarded thoughts surreptitiously roaming through my mind, I was all the while describing our Earth to Brutar. He interrupted me once. "Eo, come here."

I became aware of another shape hovering near us. It now advanced; and with Brutar's words of explanation it took form in the fashion of a young man. A smiling, deferential youth seemingly of an age just reaching maturity. He came forward meekly. Brutar spoke.

"THIS is my friend whom we call Eo. I have trust in him—he is helping me greatly. I want him to hear what you have to say, Rob."

Eo smiled again. "I hope we shall be friends." He regarded Bee, and his smile was curiously gentle. "They call you a girl? Brutar tells me what girls are—I am glad to see you."

He reclined beside Bee, continuing to regard her. A very gentle, guileless youth—how queer a companion for this Brutar! And I knew then that it was gentle beings like this whom Brutar was beguiling to his purpose.

Brutar said, "Go on, Rob. What you can tell us will be very interesting."

Particularly he questioned me about our physical bodies of Earth—the human body; and when I told him how mortal it was, how easily injured, he seemed disturbed. But only for a moment.

"I have been—well, very nearly in your Earth-state," he said. "I know how it feels. You have things with which to harm that body. Weapons—tell me of them."

I described our weapons, our warfare, our poisons. I will admit it gave me a gloating pleasure gruesomely to picture all the dangers to which our mortal flesh is heir. But outwardly he was undisturbed. He interrupted me once with a sharp admonition to Bee.

"You think you can send your thoughts back to the Big-City and guide them here, don't you? I would not try that, if I were you!"

Bee started with guilt. She had been attempting to do that. Her thoughts had gone back, at first instinctively, then with a conscious direction, but he was stopping her now. Around us, like a veil, a barrier was materializing.

Eo said gently, "She will not do that, Brutar. She is friendly to us." His hand very lightly touched Bee. He added earnestly, "I like you—girl."

Brutar momentarily had turned away; I think he was not aware of what Eo had said. I saw that Bee was smiling, I felt her voice saying very gently.

"I like you, too. You are very kind—I think you are very good. On Earth we would call you—a boy."

"Boy!" He murmured it. "I like the way that sounds—hearing you call me—boy!"

Brutar had risen erect. "You have told me a great deal, Rob. We shall be friends." He was eyeing me. "On Earth, when we get there, I shall make you into a great man—a very powerful man. You would like that?"

Did he feel that my intelligence was so limited that he could bribe me thus crudely? I smiled.

"Oh, yes—I should like that. But I've told you so much, and you haven't told me anything. How did you first find our

Earth? How did you get yourself into the Borderland, and beyond? You were the first to go, weren't you?"

"The first," he said proudly. "I discovered it—well, by accident. Shall I show you how'? And what I am doing to take all my loyal followers there with me?"

"Yes." I agreed. "That is what I want."

He led us outside. Eo walked close by Bee. I saw now that the encampment was itself one tremendous hollow globe; on Earth we would have said that it had a diameter of at least a mile. Brutar explained it proudly. Here, in the void of Space, his organized workmen had spun this huge shell of thought-matter. It was tenuous; I had not known when we passed through it coming in. Yet it was visible; within it we gazed at its interior surface. It glowed with a very pale dull light.

Upon this concave slope, in the foreground near us, were a variety of globes—small habitations for the workers. Paths ran between and over them. Further away, other larger globes glowed as though translucent, with light inside. Beyond them was a shimmering white lake—water or mist. Higher up—in the distance where the concave surface extended upward and swept back over our heads—was what seemed like dark soil. Things were growing there in orderly rows—a gigantic concave field of plants. It was quite dim off in that direction and so far above us that I could not make them out plainly.

Again, close at hand, just beyond the village of globes, was an enclosure possibly a thousand feet across. Movement was there—busy workers moving in the artificial glow of strings of lights. Vague, shifting shadows—gray shapes of men, from which the lights cast monstrous gray shadows as they moved. It seemed a dim inferno of strange industry incomprehensible... Brutar led us toward it.

"We built all this," he said; and his gesture encompassed the entire inner void within that glowing tenuous shell. "We built and poised this here in Space. My followers have forsaken their homes to join me here. Soon we will go to your Earth-realm... Some of us often go out there now—into that Borderland—to test our power."

The enclosure had a wall about it—a thick high wall built of a gray substance lying in layers, folded in convolutions. We stood upon the wall, gazing at the scene within.

"I would not have you see too much—now," Brutar said.

A cunning look was on his face. "Not—too much, until we are better friends and I can be sure of your loyalty."

THE lights were dazzling when near at hand—yet their rays carried but a little distance. I saw in the foreground beneath us, a section where men were squatting one behind the other in a long curved line. Their backs were bent forward, with heads and necks unnaturally held upright. Their arms and hands were outstretched in a curious attitude as with supplication. There must have been two hundred of the men, squatting in this single line which curved in a crescent until its end was near its beginning. They were men with bodies that seemed shrunken; their arms and hands very long; thin, tenuous. But their heads were overlarge; distorted to a swollen size.

Brutar said softly, "Now—in a moment—watch them."

A leader, raised above these squatting, motionless workmen, gave a signal. From the head of the man at the back of the line a pallid light seemed streaming. It was very faint—a glow of pale white light, no more. But as I stared, breathless, I saw that it was not exactly like light, but a stream of something moving—very faint, a fog, a mist—which a sweep of the hand might dissipate.

It streamed forward; and as it passed the head of the next man, there seemed additional light adding to it. Both men had their hands up, as though to guide the stream—gently to guide that which must have been very nearly impalpable.

But it was growing in density. Soon, further up the line with every brain contributing a share, the slowly moving stream began to have substance. From vague, luminous pallidness, it turned darker, gaining a solidity—a weight. The guiding hands sustained it, molded it, and pushed it onward.

It came to the end of the line. Other workers appeared; carried it away—a long flexible rod of newly created thought-matter. The basic inorganic substance of this work. The thickness of a man's body, it seemed coming of interminable length. Then the first worker gave out—dropped back exhausted. Then others. The rod grew tenuous and pale in places. It broke. Workers carried away the broken segments. It was not a solid yet; they molded it by their touch as they carried it away.

Another signal from the leader. The two hundred workmen, their duty done for the time, rose and departed. They moved unsteadily, exhausted. And another shift came to take their places.

How long a spell of mental work this might have been, I cannot say. Bee asked me, in an awed whisper, how long we had been watching. A futile question! As Will once said, "Like trying to add an apple to an orange." To me—idly watching and with memory of an Earth-standard of what we are pleased to call Time—I would have said five minutes. To one of those laboring workers—an eternity of effort. Yet in our fatuous little world of Earth we tick off seconds, minutes, hours, and think we are establishing a standard for the Universe!

Brutar said, "That is the crude thought-material. From there it goes to our workshops, where other minds bring it to higher, individual substances from which we make—well, we make these things we are making here."

His look of cunning came again. He would give away no secrets to me—his enemy. He seemed very proud of his cunning, this Brutar. A man of low intelligence, I realized. Yet he must be powerful, to be the leader of all this. Later I learned that he had a powerful mind—not for creating this useful substance of industry; nor was his an intellect of keen reasoning ability. Rather was it a mind powerful for the weaving of that tenuous thought-substance of combat. He was a warrior. And in mental speech as well, he was fluent, plausible, guileful.

Bee was saying, "Is all work mental?"

He did not understand the question. Eo said, "She means, is all work done by the mind?"

"Oh yes," Brutar smiled. "Why not? Except—well you've seen what part the hands play—the bodies. It is comparatively unimportant."

"May we see what they are doing with that thought-substance?" I suggested.

"No," he smiled. "I told you before, not now."

I did not press it. I was wondering if the shell of this huge globe would let me through. Could I clutch Bee and will myself away into the void? Could I not thus escape Brutar...?

My thoughts must have reached him. He said sharply, "If you regard the welfare of your mind, Rob, you will not attempt to wander." His tone changed to a menacing contempt. "I can strike that sickly mind of yours from your body in an instant. Have care!"

I fancied I caught a warning glance from Eo. Bee gave a low half-suppressed cry of fear. I smiled at Brutar.

"You are too suspicious," I said. "If we are to be friends you go about it badly."

He did not answer that, and I added, "You said you would tell us how you discovered our Earth-realm. It must have seemed an extraordinary discovery."

His vanity was easily touched. He smiled again.

"Yes, I will tell you. And show you. It is no secret—that leader, Thone, of the Big-City knows it... So I do not mind showing you."

CHAPTER THIRTEEN
The Lolos Flower

WE stepped back from the wall. Brutar led us onward through the twilight. We passed globes translucent with light from within; heard the hum and hiss of work going on—but Brutar would not let us enter. We passed a dark bowl of enormous size, like a great globe cut in half. We encircled its rim. I stared down into darkness; gray shapes of inert things were ranged there—things that had been manufactured of the thought-substance, I surmised. But Brutar would not say.

We skirted the misty lake. It seemed a blanket of fog lying there. Within me, at the sight, a vague pang stirred. A desire—unpleasant in its suggestion of a needed gratification; and with it a premonition of coming pleasure.

I was puzzled. There was no instinct to warn me; or if there was, my puzzled reason subverted it. I described my feeling to Eo.

"It seems physical," I said. "I had forgotten my body—but there seems a pang there."

"Thirst," he said readily. The word he used gave me the thought of thirst. And this was water, or its equivalent.

I knelt beside the white layers of mist. Did I inhale it, or drink it? I have no means of knowing; but I know that the pang left me, and that the experience was vaguely pleasant.

We moved on and came at last to the great field. Behind us the opposite side of the encampment—the enclosure wherein I had seen the creation of thought-material—was now almost over our heads. The ground of the field was soft and flaky—it seemed as though it might have been a black soil lying in flakes. Things were rooted within it—growing things set in long orderly rows that stretched up the concave surface into the dimness of distance. They appeared to be plants, in height about to my knee with a central stalk and branches bent outward like gesturing arms. A bud, or flower, at the top. It seemed to carry features—a face. My imagination? Something that had been said or suggested to me? Possibly. But the things bent aside as we advanced upon them. They seemed eyeing us; suddenly I was conscious of a myriad of eyes from everywhere fixed upon me.

I said to Brutar, "This black ground—is that thought-material?"

"Yes," he said. "Made from the same substance you saw created. But many mental processes were necessary to bring it to this final state."

"And then you planted these—things in it?" I asked. "They look as though they had an intelligence. I don't understand that. Are they growing here—or what?"

Brutar hesitated. I think that the man's learning was not very great. Eo said:

"I believe I can explain it, Rob. All things in our world are divided into two classes. One—the inert, material bodies. These we create from nothingness to their final perfected state. The other class—living organisms—is very different. The addition of a Creator—thought is necessary. These plants—to be specific—are called lolos. The lolos plant. To create it we must have a spore—an infinitesimal something already existing. With this spore, others like it may be created by our own mentalities. And nurtured by our mentalities through a period of growth. But that latter process can be simplified by the production of this soil in which the plants are then nourished. It is basically an identical process."

"IT is much like our own world," I said. "Except that these plants seem to have a conscious mind."

"Why not?" Brutar demanded. "Every living thing has a mind."

Eo added, "Since the essence of everything is mentality—naturally the spark of life must bring that mentality to consciousness."

"These things then," I said, "they know that they are alive?"

"Of course. And Rob, what you told Brutar of your Earth-agriculture—what you called your vegetable kingdom—seems not so very different from ours."

"But it is different," I said. "Our plants—our growing things—are not aware that they are alive."

Eo demanded gently, "How do you know that? Is it not perhaps that your own mentality is lacking, to gauge the power of theirs?"

I smiled. "It may be so... Brutar, these lolos plants—what is their purpose?"

"With them we are going to your Earth," he said. "This lolos plant of itself has a power very wonderful. We crush it; and the blood of it taken into our body, sends the mind upon strange and pleasant wanderings."

"Evil wanderings," said Eo.

A drug! As Brutar further explained, I realized it. And I wondered if this lolos plant—the name of it—sounded thus since to my own mentality it suggested the lotus flower. I think that was so.

The blood of this plant was a powerful narcotic. Brutar had been addicted to its use and his wandering mind had come into the Borderland. He had seen our Earth-realm and gone further until he experienced the sensations of our physical consciousness. He had come back, to gather his followers, to create in quantity the blood of this lolos that all might go to conquer and enjoy this greater realm.

Brutar was absorbed in his subject. Listening to him, I had nevertheless noticed that Bee's attention was fixed upon Eo. She was whispering to him. With his sweet, boyish face, he was listening to her, enraptured. He was close beside her, and I saw that he was touching her. Brutar, still talking to me, bent to show me one of the lolos plants. It shrank away from him as though in fear. He frowned; struck it a blow with his hand. His attention momentarily was diverted from us. I heard Eo murmur softly, yet tensely.

"You are right—girl. This is evil—I realize it now... Rob! Hold yourself firm! Stay with me! We will try to escape..."

I MUST revert now to Will, Thone and Ala in the Big-City. They had felt Bee's thoughts; they knew we were in danger; Ala had caught just enough to know that we were with Brutar.

"We must go," Thone hastily declared. "Try and follow them, Ala. That Brutar is a mind very powerful for evil."

With Will held firmly between them, they swept out into space. To Will it was a dream, a nightmare of mental chaos. Rushing through the dark—through seemingly endless Space for endless Time. But he saw none of the distorted things that I had seen, for he was in friendly hands. A rushing black Nothingness sweeping past. A vague dream of flight; but presently he found his mind clearing.

The void was illimitable. But soon it seemed not wholly empty. To one side was a faint glow—an infinite distance away, as though it might have been a nebula gleaming over Space a thousand million light-years of distance. Or something shining from another Time-eons away. It moved sidewise as they swept along. It glowed, faded, and was gone.

"We will not go there." Ala murmured. She seemed to shudder. "That is the Realm of Disease. I hope never to go there."

Endless Time passing. Or perhaps, as Will was thinking, Time was in abeyance, standing still, non-existent.

And Will saw other far-off gleaming patches, like faint drifting stardust. Soon they were gone. He did not ask what they might be.

Ala still felt Bee's thoughts. Then they ceased. Will became aware of a confusion, a fluttering, as though now the flight had lost direction. He gazed around intently, searchingly, but the space at that moment was wholly empty.

"Where are we?" he asked.

Thone and Ala were exchanging thoughts. Thone said:

"Where are we? There is no answer, Will. There is nothing here. We are nowhere."

A confusion. It seemed that Ala and Thone felt that Brutar's self-created world might be found by approaching the Realm of Disease. Will waited, listening silently while they talked of it...

Abruptly Will saw something—a blur, a vague luminosity beneath them. It was moving. Suddenly he knew it was not large and faraway, but small and very close. It mounted, broke visually apart, and resolved itself into two dark blobs—shapes. The moving shapes of a man and a woman.

They came nearer. The woman was Bee! It was Bee and the youthful Eo. He was clinging to her; she seemed helping him struggle upward.

They reached Will. Bee gasped. "He—he is hurt! Oh Will—it's you. Help him—his mind struggles to leave us. He is wounded. I think—I think he is going to die!"

She seemed crying as she flung herself into Will's arms. "I don't want him to die He is my friend—so gentle, so lovable—I don't want him to die!"

CHAPTER FOURTEEN
The Realm of Death

I MUST tell again of that moment when we—Bee and I—were standing beside the lolos field with Brutar and Eo. Brutar had turned away. Eo—prompted, I had no doubt, by Bee—murmured, "This is evil! We will escape—"

My arm reached for Bee. I told myself intensely that now we must escape...now I must fling my thoughts—my mind—out into the void and stay with Eo. He would lead us.

I think my groping hand never reached Bee. I felt a swishing sound. A swirl of thoughts struck me—like feathers blown against me in a gale. But they seemed to cling—invisible, imponderable, barely palpable. Dimly I could feel these thoughts like a net entangling me.

I was floundering. Surging through blackness. Where was Bee? I thought I saw her and Eo whirling near me. But it was a thought unreal—hallucination; for as I tried to grip it and make them visible, they were gone. My thought of them dissolved into a realization that I did not see them, for they were vanished.

But Brutar I saw; a distorted wraith of him...his grim, menacing face...grim with combat...

I was rushing through blackness. But as an undertow may suck the strongest swimmer, something was pulling me back...a hampering net around me...materializing into greater ponderability...holding me firmly. The blackness about me was taking form. I strove to think I saw the Big-City. I told myself that that hovering shape above me was Thone—the friendly Thone; not Brutar.

But it was not Thone; and this place that was clarifying to my vision was not the Big-City. The lolos field! I came—was dragged, sucked back to it! The lolos field—I was standing there where before I had been. And the menacing shape was Brutar—my captor standing there grimly confronting me.

But Bee and Eo were gone.

These two, escaping, came upon Thone, Will and Ala as I have related. Came upon them hovering nowhere in the void. Eo was stricken. Brutar, with what quickness and evil power of mind I could not conceive, had struck at Eo. A wound, a derangement not physical, but mental. His mind now sick, stricken with disease. Almost wandering, yet not quite unhinged, for the power of his will was holding it. Bravely he clung to sanity. Fought for it. Yet those—his friends with him—knew then that he fought a losing battle.

They hung there in the void. Bee was sobbing. "I don't want him to die! He is my friend."

He held tightly to her. His eyes were very wistful. "They call you a girl—and now I know I love you!"

The void was moving. It seemed so to Will; seemed that the blackness was moving past them. Or was it that they—the little knot of their hovering shapes—was moving? Then Will realized that it was Eo—his stricken, wandering mind—dragging them somewhere. The void seemed moving—for how long Will did not know. And then, far away, in Space and in eons of Time, something became visible. A faint stardust glow. A luminous patch. It broadened; spread to the sides, and up and down until everywhere before them lay its gleaming radiance.

The realm of disease! Will heard Ala murmur it in accents of sorrow and apprehension. Eo was rushing for it—and no power that they had could stop him.

The radiance intensified. A fear—a shuddering horror possessed Will. With every instinct within him, he recoiled from the approach. Revolted. But he held tightly to Thone and to Bee; told himself that they would lead him safely.

Everything was glowing; they were wholly within the glow now. A silvery glow that shone everywhere about them. But soon to the silver there came a greenish caste. It deepened. A green, with its sickly look of death. Green, with the silver turning to a pallid, flat, dead whiteness. And then a mingled brown, a murk, like a fog pervading everything.

Abruptly Will became conscious that Eo was no longer with them. His last despairing cry; and Bee's echo. He was going, floating downward; while they—uncontaminated— hovered above at the edge of the realm, to see it but not to enter.

Will saw but dimly. Saw shapes floating in there. Dismembered shapes. Others, whole, floating inert. A caldron, with bubbles of sight and sound, and smell. Shrouded in murk. Unreal… A wailing…sobbing…faint aerial voices wailing like ghosts distraught… And a stench— the thought of it, no more—but to Will the thought, the knowledge of all this was horrible, fearsome. Singularly fearsome; above everything at that moment he feared this realm, this state of unnatural, tortured existence…

They could still talk to Eo. See him there, laboring, losing his brave fight to come back to them. He seemed very far away; and yet very close, for though his form was down there, engulfed with all the leprous horrors of disease, his voice was very plainly heard. And his face, the image of it, the physical representation of it to Will's thought, seemed again at hand. His eyes were very wistful. He was smiling gently at Bee.

"Soon, girl, I will be gone—into death—it is very near now. I can see it—see it, just ahead…"

Will saw it, too. Another realm beyond the one they were skirting. The realm of death. It lay close ahead—dark, mysterious, scarce to be seen, but only imagined.

Again came Eo's faint voice. "I shall—be there in a moment. It is very—beautiful. I can see it—right here—" And then he suddenly whispered, "I love you, my girl Bee—"

And vanished.

OR DID HE vanish? The shell of him then seemed lying in Bee's arms. But it was an empty nothing; the shell of a shape of something which once had been, but now was not…

Thone said gravely, "Watch it, Will, the Thought is gone from it. Our own thought-matter is all that is left. You shall see of what permanence that is."

The dead shell lay inert. It was dissolving… Gruesome… Will turned away, then forced his vision back to see a leprous wraith—a rotting shape which presently, like a melting fog, began to dissipate. Dissolving…until the very last essence of it was gone into nothingness.

Ala seemed to sigh. "It is very horrible. Yet I think that we are wrong to consider it so, for it is Nature."

Will recovered himself. The realm of disease had withdrawn to a memory. Around him the blackness seemed purified. But ahead he could see—or thought he saw—that other endless realm where dwell what we call the dead. Questions flooded him. Eo was there? Could they not go and see him? Could he—this entity which lad once been Eo—could he not still speak to them from beyond the borders of death?

Thone said, "We will approach it if you wish."

Unnamable time; and then Will found that they were there, hovering; and a realm, a place—a something he knew not what—lay spread above them. Earnestly he groped for it, not with his physical hands but with his senses. His thought went there and back. He thought he saw shapes up there. Hovering, glowing shapes in a great light space. And with futile, childish imagination he endowed them with beautiful, ethereal qualities; transfigured them into glowing human shapes of beauty and peace. And thought he saw them; and that they might speak to him. Or that perhaps, because Thone might be more than human, they might communicate with Thone, and thence to him.

And then he laughed. It was all so childish!

Thone said, "Eo is there, in the darkness and the light. You can think of him. Your thought will go there. And it will come back to you, fraught with what qualities your imagination may lend it. But nothing else."

"No," said Will, "nothing else, understand that now."

CHAPTER FIFTEEN
The Birth of a Thought

THEY TURNED away in the void—away from the dark-light mystery of the realm of death, and drove themselves back to the Big-City. The search for Brutar's encampment was at the moment futile; they knew they could not reach it. And though Bee had escaped with Eo, she did not know whether I escaped or not.

They hoped to find me safely returned to the Big-City, but I was not there. But still Thone felt that I might come. To Will—with his inherent, instinctive conception of a placid, measured Time—the delay seemed dangerous. He was impatient, anxious to do something. But there was nothing that of himself he could do, and Thone was an intelligence very keen. Will decided that upon Thone he must rely.

They went back to the home globe, to rest and to wait for my possible arrival. Will in a way was glad of the inactivity, for he remembered that of Thone's plans he knew almost nothing. He would learn all he could, and with something definitely arranged, they could act to better purpose.

Will felt the pangs of hunger. They brought a glowing brazier wherein something smoldered. He ate (inhaled, there is no word for it) and satisfied his pangs, then drank of the silver mist, which came flowing into the globe at a word of command. He then slept, lost consciousness, to then find himself in blackness with Time wholly gone.

But still I did not come back to the Big-City. There were times when with Thone, Will journeyed about the city streets, gazing at this strange life. He saw thought-workers, as I had seen them in Brutar's encampment. Saw the water being created; saw the thought-matter molded and spun into new globes—molded to all the diverse purposes of this Ego-life.

He slept again; several times; and ministered to the slight wants of his tenuous body. A great length of time seemed passing; and still I did not arrive.

There were many talks that Will had with Thone. Ala and Bee were generally there, as befitted those of their sex.

Sex? It was interesting to Will. The creation of the individual Ego of this strange realm, so different an existence, and yet in fundamental conception so like his own. Already he believed that the same Creator governed both. With strange ways that we mortals so little understand, over all the realms, the states of existence, the Universes that possibly could exist—only one Creator held sway. The thought—there could be but One.

Will said, "You once spoke, Thone, of yourself as Ala's parent. And the necessity of the thought to the creation of Ego life. Will you explain that? In our world we have two sexes. Have you also?"

"Yes," said Thone. "In the higher forms of life—we humans, as you would say—there are, like yours, two sexes. Call me a man—and Ala a woman. The difference is one of mental capacity, mental qualities, inherent perhaps to the Ego. I call it the soul, though we have no name for it. I mean that certain something that makes each individual different from every other.

"The qualities inherent to the individual mould and form the mentality. Characterize thus, what we call its sex. The one sex is a complement to the other. An attraction exists between them—a desire for proximity so that of their own inherent force they will draw together. And the one mentality derives force—a mental life-force—from the other. An exchange—for it yields its own necessary qualities in return. Thus we have the mating—the basis of the family. Without it no complete mental health is possible. There is no mentality capable of existing in health by itself."

"AND A birth?" Will suggested.

"Communion of thought. The desire, the longing of two closely interwoven mentalities of complementary qualities. When they combine with an intensity of longing, the thought-matter they mutually create brings into existence another, smaller shape like themselves. It is very small—very tenuous—scarce to be seen save by those two who have produced it. It lies inert. Almost formless, though they sit beside it and strive with their loving thoughts of what it should be—strive to give it form. It may continue to lie inert; and at last in spite of their efforts, it may dissolve, dissipate— be gone, back into nothingness from whence they drew it. The Thought was not within it; it never was anything then save a human longing unblessed.

"Or again, the Thought may be there. It lives. Grows ponderable. Moves of itself. Thinks of itself. Then it *is*

something itself—something independent of all save its cre-
ator-divine... The little nourishment of its body is easily
supplied; the mother-parent gives it lovingly the needed
gentler nourishment of the mind; daily she adds to it the
loving tendrils of her thought-matter so tenuous that to the
sight it seems mere light.

"But if the spark is there, glowing brightly, the little Ego
lives. Grows in size. Displays a growing mental capacity of
its own. Its own mental qualities make themselves known, to
identify it as a man-child, or a woman-child. And the Ego,
developing, brings it to individuality. It is itself, unlike
everyone else. The new Individual... That, my friend Will, is
a birth."

Will thought a moment. "There is a beauty to it."

Bee said, "I don't quite understand—" She gazed at Will,
puzzled; and Will felt and understood her confusion. He
said:

"Your explanation Thone, seems to make Man differ from
Woman only in qualities of the Soul and Mind. You do not
speak of the body; yet to me, Ala here appears of very
different form from yourself."

Thone smiled. "You say, 'to me.' You have answered
yourself, my friend. The physical aspect of everything is but
the reflected image of it within our own mentality. The
gentleness of Ala—those qualities that make her what she
is—are seen by you in the form of what you call a woman."

"But," protested Will, "does she not look the same to
you?"

"THAT I do not know," he returned earnestly. "Nor do
you. We can only see, think, imagine for ourselves. Our
conscious universe is our own; it exists of our own creation,
and what it is of itself apart from us, I do not know."

"We have on Earth," Will said, "a school of philosophical thinking which believes that nothing exists apart from the mentality perceiving it. Believes that without a consciousness of existence, nothing can exist."

"That may be so," Thone replied gravely.

Bee was still puzzled. She said to Thone, "Ala, to me, looks different from you. She looks, as Will says, like a girl. Won't you tell us how she looks to you?"

He thought a moment. "She looks—like Ala," he said slowly. "I think we mould our images from the individual itself—not upon a generality of sex. She looks to me like Ala, as I know her to be. Very gentle. Very keen of reasoning. Very quick—" He smiled. "Yet not always so very logical. She looks like the Ala of my creation—mine and that other mentality whom you would call her mother—" His voice turned solemn, with a singular hush to it. "Her mother—who has long since gone into that realm of mystery."

At other times they talked of practical subjects. Brutar's coming invasion of Earth; my own fate, since I still was missing, unheard from. And they talked of what could be done to overcome Brutar and his horde of followers.

Thone, it seemed to Will, had accomplished very little. He had learned of Brutar's purpose and of the establishment of his realm. Thone had sent—by the aid of the lolos plant—an adventurer into the Borderland who had seen Brutar and some of his cohorts experimenting with the Earth-state. Then Ala had gone into the Borderland; had met Will; had arranged to bring him, Bee and myself back to see her parent.

Little of accomplishment! A public meeting of protest, which we had attended, and which Brutar invaded. But now Thone was organizing his Thinkers—his army, as it might have been called on Earth. Their purpose was to seek out Brutar's realm by concerted effort of thought; to find it while Brutar's preparations were still incomplete, and to destroy it.

The very conception of warfare of this kind was difficult for Will to encompass. There were no weapons—nothing of the sort we on Earth would call weapons. Will showed Thone his broad belt, and the contents of its pouches. He drew out a revolver and a knife. Thone inspected them curiously—shadowy, glowing objects which almost floated when tossed into the air, so imponderable were they.

Will explained their Earthly uses. He said, a trifle shamefacedly, "I brought them—but I felt they would be of no advantage here."

He pulled the trigger of the revolver. If it discharged, there was no result which his Ego-senses could perceive. Thone said, handing him the knife, "Strike me with it."

The action was instinctively revolting; yet Will drove the knife blade into the semblance of Thone's arm. Thone said, "It seems to hurt."

To Will the knife might have been a feather he was thrusting against a pillow. He withdrew the blade; fancied he saw in Thone's arm an open gash. But if he did, the gash closed at once. The outlines of the arm were quivering, unreal, under Will's earnest gaze. And he knew that if he persisted in regarding it, the arm would turn formless to his sight.

He exclaimed, "Useless! Of course." And tossed the knife away. But Thone recovered it. "In the Borderland it would be more effective, Will. Keep it."

Thone explained how his army of Thinkers might destroy Brutar's encampment. The thought-matter, created, was held in substance only by continued mental effort. And this withdrawn, at once the disintegrating forces of Nature would dissolve it into nothingness.

"So it is," Thone said, "when an Ego dies. The persistent, subconscious effort of mind during life is all that holds the shell of body in existence. Withdraw that—and you have dissolution."

"And with inorganic matter—" Will began.

"With this globe, for instance," said Thone. "With everything we have created, a worker-mentality must guard it. Replenish it."

To Will that seemed not very strange. "On Earth," he said, "we must repair. Nature slowly but steadily tears down that which we have built."

"OF COURSE," Thone responded. "We will destroy Brutar's encampment, himself, and all his followers. Rather should I say, we will force them to stop replenishing—and Nature will destroy."

Then Will said, "Let me ask you this: I understand that if you, with you weaving of the net of thoughts, are quicker, more powerful than I, you will beat down my resistance. Entrap me; force my body to follow you."

"Or to depart from me," Thone added. "I could force you back—as far from me as I could spin the net."

"I was thinking—suppose we must fight them in the Borderland—"

"A combat at once physical and mental," Thone retorted. He smiled. "You think we are ill-prepared, Will? That is not so. My men of Science have studied this condition—experimented with it very fully. The Borderland—the transition into your Earth-state—all such things are new to us. But we are coming to understand them, and I think that Brutar's people know little of their subject…"

He paused in contemplation; then went on slowly. "We are not sure how permanent may be the transition by the lolos—blood into the state of your Earth-matter. Brutar may be mistaken in that—"

He paused again. His smile had a gleam of irony, and there came into his voice an ironic note. "I am not sure but that from the Borderland, our opposing thoughts might not reach your Earth-state. They might, perhaps, do strange things to those of Brutar's people who have reached there— who have taken with them what they may think are effective weapons."

That Thone had learned, or divined much of Brutar's purpose, and that he was prepared to combat it, was evident. But at the moment he chose to speak no further. He added abruptly, "My Thinkers are organized. Very soon they will be ready. The mind, my friend Will, grows strong only with use. Every moment that they can, they are developing the strength of battle... Come here and see."

They passed upward upon the side of the globe; and at once its opaque wall began to glow; become translucent; transparent, until through it Will saw the city. An open space, from this angle seemingly tilted on end, was nearby. Within it a horde of shapes was squatting. Figures which after a moment of inspection seemed men—gaunt of body, but with craniums distended. A horde, a myriad—Will could not have guessed at their number. Squatting in a giant spiral, curving inward to its center point. From the heads of them all light was streaming. It spun in a band close over them; whirled, flashed with iridescent color. A spiral band of light, concentrating at the center point into a beam that shot away and was lost in the darkness.

The globe wall became again opaque; the scene vanished. Thone said softly, "There is much power for combat in mentalities like those. And very soon I will put them to searching for Brutar's realm..."

A cry from Ala interrupted him. The girl had been seated as though in meditation; but now she flung herself erect.

"I can find this encampment of Brutar—I can lead you to it now!"

Thone stared.

"Are you getting thoughts from it?" Will demanded eagerly. And Bee gave a glad exclamation. She asked, "Is Rob there? Is he safe, Ala? Can you take us to him?"

"I do not know if he is there, or safe. Oh, I cannot tell you those things! I only know I can take you to Brutar's realm!"

"You feel no thoughts from there?" said Thone.

"No."

Thone was standing with the others. No delay now. He was ready. He said to Will, "It is the nameless power. Those only whom you call women have it."

"Intuition," Will supplied.

"We say, the nameless... You may try, Ala. And, if once you take me there—" A restrained, grave triumph was upon him.

"Once I have been there, with perfect sureness I can lead our Thinkers to the attack."

Again in the void... The power of woman's mentality— the nameless power; illogical, against all reason, all science; not to be explained... But it was leading them... A rush through the darkness of vague, unreasoning woman's thought; a distance, a time felt, but immeasurable; a direction not to be fathomed... And then, ahead of them as in a clinging group they followed Ala, the glow of a poised realm became visible. They neared it; hovered in the void regarding it. And they knew and saw that it was Brutar's realm—that great, tenuous globe, hanging there like a gigantic bubble. They could see within it; see details as though by some magnification the details were close at hand.

The encampment was deserted! Abandoned! The lolos field was uprooted, its plants gone. The globes, the workshops, the streets, the fields—all were deserted. And more than that, with the removal of all conscious, constructive, replenishing mentality, disintegration already was taking place. A leprous realm. Holes of Nothingness were visibly eating their way into everything. Rotting walls...rotting habitations...

Under the gaze of the watchers the whole realm was melting. Dissolving into slow-flowing viscosity; cesspools of putridity, rising into mists, vapors—a puff of Nothingness...

The realm was vanished. The void was black, empty and silent. The little group of apprehensive watchers turned away.

Brutar—presumably taking me with him—had already started his invasion of Earth!

CHAPTER SIXTEEN
The March of the Ghosts

I REMAINED a captive of Brutar, and at length the time came when he was ready to start his conquest of Earth. His army, his followers, quietly had departed from the encampment and were waiting for him in the Borderland. He stood before me—we two the last living minds remaining in his self-created realm. Around me I could see it even then beginning to rot and crumble.

He said, "The blood of the lolos is ready for us, Rob. But before we start I will warn you—if once more you try to escape you will be killed." I could not doubt but that he spoke his true intent.

He brought then a bowl, or brazier, in which like food, the dried burning blood of the lolos was glowing. It was a dull red in the gloom, with tiny green tongues licking upward from it. I could not see the smoke. But I could sense it—smell it. We reclined by the brazier. The fumes brought a reeling of my senses.   Unpleasant, frightening... Then pleasant indeed. A drowsy drifting into rosy vacancy. I had intended not to yield myself wholly, but my will weakened... I told myself that Brutar would guide me...

Out of the darkness at last with returning consciousness I found a gentle net of Brutar's thoughts cradling me. And himself regarding me impatiently.

"Come, Rob. We are here. Stay close by me—and if you help me as I wish, reward shall be yours."

There was a tenseness to his voice. I gazed around. We were in the Borderland—that same dark void with its roiling slopes. Near at hand I saw some two hundred of Brutar's workers—his fighters—drawn up in orderly array. Shadows like myself. And behind them a rabble of Egos in the fashion of men, women and children. His followers, waiting to enter the Earth-realm when the fighters had conquered it.

I saw, too, hovering near Brutar and me, a dozen shapes of men—the leaders of Brutar's army awaiting his instructions.

When I was more fully alert. Brutar drew me aside. He spoke with a new force and succinctness. Because now the time for action had come and I think also that as we neared our Earth-state, there was a tendency toward restoration of all Earthly qualities.

"Rob," he said, "I'll tell you now my plan. Your greatest city is near at hand—somewhere near here."

"New York," I said.

"Yes. I plan to attack it—demolish it. It's a very small portion of your Earth, of course, but with that evidence of my power I think your Earth-leaders will cease to fight me— will admit my supremacy. If not—well, then I shall demolish each of your great cities in turn—"

He told me then that these two hundred men, along with his dozen sub-leaders, were all the fighting force he at first proposed to use. We were about to attack New York City. His people would wait, here in the Borderland, for our success; then would enter the Earth-state to take possession of it.

"You can help me, Rob, because you know your city better than I do. Look around us now—tell me exactly, where are we?"

I saw then the shadows of ghostly houses. My own world! Gray, spectral houses...streets...a church...trees lining a street of residences in a small quiet town. It lay in a plane tilted at a slight angle, and perhaps thirty feet above us. I looked up to the street overhead. Quiet? It was thronged with people—ghostly shapes crowded up there staring down at us. It seemed to be night up there. I could see the streetlights, spots of light in the houses, and the headlights of scurrying automobiles.

The town was in a turmoil. I knew that its people saw us down here as a myriad half-materialized ghosts. They were crowding to watch us. They realized that now at last the ghosts had come in a horde! Perhaps to attack. I saw policemen on the streets; and presently a company of soldiers came along. Spurts of flame showed as evidently they fired tentatively toward the ground. But there was no sound.

Brutar chuckled. "Well, they're really frightened now! And they have cause to be. Where are we, Rob?"

It seemed possibly a suburb of New York City. I did not recognize it at once. Then off to one side I saw a shadowy river, with ghostly cliffs on its further bank. The Hudson!

"I don't know where we are," I said carefully. "Where do you want to go first, Brutar?"

"To New York City—down there where there is river all around, and a great pile of buildings."

Lower New York. But I would not lead him. I protested ignorance.

A shape approached us, a man. He gestured. "I know it is that way, Brutar."

We started. The two hundred fighters in a triple file came after us. Brutar had ordered the mob of men and women to wait where they were. We advanced slowly, and I saw with sinking heart that we were going southward. Upper New York City soon lay close ahead.

IT WAS A strange, soundless march. The slopes of the Borderland carried us sometimes above, and sometimes below the ground of Earth. But generally we were below it. Up there over our heads the shadowy landscape was silently slipping backward. It was all too familiar now. We were under upper Broadway. Huge apartment houses loomed high up there, with the Hudson almost at our level to the right.

Our advance was followed up above. From every window people were peering fearsomely down at us. The cross streets were jammed. But ahead of us policemen were clearing them. And down empty Broadway, and down each of the North and South Avenues troops of the State Militia were marching, keeping as nearly as possible directly over us.

"Brutar," I said, "you cannot fight this world. Look at them there. They're ready—waiting."

Machine guns were posted at most of the street corners now; and as we passed beneath them they were moved swiftly forward to other streets ahead of us. The boat traffic of the river was being cleared. Police boats, armed and ready, were paralleling our march. A war-vessel lay anchored ahead, off Grant's Tomb. Its funnels were smoking, and as we neared it, very slowly it steamed along with us.

And over in Jersey and on Long Island I had no doubt they were ready with watching troops and every precaution. Let one of us who now were mere ghosts dare to materialize further, and at once we would be killed. What could Brutar do?

He laughed at my thoughts. "You shall see, Rob, when we get among the great houses and I lay my weapons."

I could not fathom what he meant, but the sure confidence of his tone had an ominous ring to it. Weapons? I saw none. We were empty-handed, Brutar and I. And the twelve sub-leaders were empty-handed as well. But of Brutar's attacking force marching behind us, I had noticed that each man was carrying a single article. I could not call them weapons; I did not know what they were. They seemed more like gray, ghostly bricks, each man carrying one.

What were they? I could no more than guess. Some material, doubtless of Brutar's creation, brought into this Borderland state. Would these ghosts—each with a simple brick like these—would they dare to materialize, dare to enter our Earth-state upon an equality of being with the armed, massed troops awaiting them? It seemed incredible. Two hundred ghosts marching in spectral array beneath the city, with soldiers above; and machine guns, and war vessels alert to destroy them.

I told myself that there was nothing to fear. I had thought of escape. Desperately I would try to rejoin Will and Bee that we might do something to stem this invasion. Or escape, and get up there to Earth, to tell the authorities what I knew. But sober reason told me that as yet I knew very little. I had best stay with Brutar, to learn what I could.

We passed under the length of Manhattan, came at last to lower Broadway. We were close beneath it. The great shadowy piles of masonry towered above us. Looking upward I could see the shadowy outlines of the foundations of the buildings; to the right the tubes leading to New Jersey beneath the river; the network of water mains; gas; light; arteries of the city. And I could see up through the subcellars, the cellars, and into the buildings themselves. Towering structures with all their anatomy laid bare as though some giant X-ray were turned upon them.

We stopped; gathered in a group. We were just beneath City Hall Park, standing partly within one of the Subway tunnels. No trains were running. Soldiers were massed on the station platform. They came along the tracks-transparent ghosts of uniformed, armed men—came until some of them passed directly through us; and stood nearby, grimly watching and waiting.

In the empty park overhead, policemen were on guard, and troops were bringing in machine guns. I could see, too, that soldiers were now massing on the shadowy Brooklyn Bridge; police boats were clustering on the river there; and armed men were waiting in the cellar of every building nearby. There were towering giants of buildings all about us here... The Woolworth Building was close at hand...

Brutar said, "I should not care just now, to materialize further, Rob. These men look very determined." His laugh was ironical. "They are watching us closely—much good it will do them!"

He called his little band of fighters to him; they stood partly on the Subway tracks and partly beneath them. And he gave his low-toned instructions.

I saw ten of his men move aside as he indicated them. "Yes," he said. "You first. And I think I would work upon that large house over there."

Silently, with their ghostly glowing bricks in hand, the ten advanced. Across the Subway tracks, through the spectral earth and rock strata under Broadway. Climbing or floating upward, I could not tell. Moving through and into the vitals of the Woolworth Building.

CHAPTER SEVENTEEN
The Attacking Spectres

I SAID to Brutar, "You asked my help. But you have let me do nothing to help you—and you explain nothing, so that I have no idea what is going on. Am I not enough your friend by now?"

Brutar smiled; I think he was fatuous enough to believe that he had won me over.

"You will be able to help me, Rob. We're going to place these weapons everywhere. There is a statue near here somewhere—a giant figure rising from water. I want you to lead us to it. Later—when we have finished with this great house."

"Weapons?" I echoed. "What sort of weapons?"

He continued to smile. "You called them bricks a while ago. That's what they are—inert material we brought with us. I had devised other things, but thought that these would suffice. Come here—I'll show you."

He took one of the bricks. As I stood with him to examine it, a score of the ghostly troopers came across the Subway tracks and fronted us.

It was a light substance, but quite ponderable. It was solid, yet rather of the consistency of soft rubber. I seemed to be able to mould its shape slightly with my fingers. Blue-green of color or silver phosphorescence; and it glowed and shimmered in my hands.

I gave it back to Brutar. "You're going to place these—where?"

"Everywhere," he said. "You shall see. Let us go watch my men place them up there in the great house... This fellow is very bold! He doesn't seem afraid of me!"

He strode vigorously at the intent and curious soldier—passed through him; but the soldier did not move.

"Come, Rob—let's go up and watch them."

We moved under the Woolworth Building, up to and through the bottoms of its great elevator shafts. And climbing—upon what I cannot say or guess—we passed upward and into the building. Through its walls; its skeleton framework of steel; floating back and forth through its many storied offices... Roaming ghosts!

The ten ghosts of Brutar were floating silently about. We ourselves could be seen by those within the building—seen as spectres hovering, moving with what silent, sinister purpose they did not know.

Yet they tried to resist us. We came, for instance, upon one of Brutar's men, with the brick still in his hand.

"Shall I place it here?" he asked. "We have chosen this side—I thought this might be a good spot."

We were some four stories above ground. Before us was one of the great upright girders of the structure.

"I should think so," Brutar agreed. The man held the glowing, oblong brick within the shadowy steel. He released it, and it floated gently downward—wafted down like a feather very slowly. But it kept within the outlines of the girder.

"You'd better follow it," said Brutar. "It will stop presently—and perhaps where you want it."

Inside the building the Earth-people had seen us—we three hovering there. Men and soldiers were running from room to room, and up and down the staircases trying to get near us. There was a room and a portion of a hallway close to where we now hovered. They were soon thronged with men, crowding against the walls, within which our white shapes were visible. But the walls, solid to them, stopped their advance. They stood regarding us; and now I could see fear upon their faces as their glances followed the downward floating brick. And as it descended a story, many of them rushed down, scrambling against the walls, striving to reach into the place where they saw it.

Did they divine its purpose? I thought so. For as presently it came to rest—lodged in the upright steel where cross girders were riveted—I saw men come rushing with crowbars and axes. Frantically they were tearing at the walls, ripping out the wood and plaster, striving to reach and perhaps to dislodge that shimmering thing lying there in the vitals of the building.

Brutar laughed. "You see, Rob? They're beginning to understand now—and they're frightened. *It is materializing*—that brick, as you call it, is materializing!"

Growing solid! In a surging torrent of horror complete realization rushed over me. I scarce heard Brutar's gloating words: "That inert matter, freed of physical contact with our Borderland bodies, tends slowly to change to the state of the thing nearest to it. As heat by contact communicates, so does the vibratory rate of all substances. That brick, lodged there, is materializing. Slowly now—but soon very fast. Presently it will be as solid as the steel girder itself—a brick resting there complete in your Earth-state—demanding space of its own, for its own existence!"

SPACE of its own! What diabolical force of Nature would this unleash! These molecules, atoms, electrons of the steel and brick thus intermingled! In a Space but half sufficient! A force created of unknown, unthinkable power—immeasurable as that proverbial irresistible force meeting an immovable body. Two solid bodies here, intermingled to their very essence, striving to occupy the same space at the same time!

Brutar was drawing at me. "Look at them, Rob! Trying to get at it! And up there—and down below—see them?"

The glowing bricks were lodged up and down the building—all seemingly on the one side. Down underground, lodged in the very foundations of the structure I could see three of them piled together. And frantic shapes of men digging for them through the walls of the cellars.

"Come further away, Rob. We can see it better from a distance. It should be very interesting."

We retreated, going back until again we were standing just beneath the level of City Hall Park. Brutar's men gathered around us—two hundred ghosts clustered there watching the fruit of their diabolical efforts. There were soldiers with machine guns in the park. The guns impotently, ridiculously were trained upon us. And around the edge of the park a cordon of police kept back the crowds. I wondered what time of night it might be. Evening, possibly; and then I saw the spectral clock of the little tower of the squat City Hall. It was just before midnight.

Our march, perhaps not so much sinister as weird to the public, had drawn a jam of the morbidly curious to this part of the city. They were packed everywhere. And all the normal activities of the city were stopped. No traffic en the streets. Vehicles motionless.

The great Woolworth Building stood like the ghost of some grave giant, serene, majestic in the power of its size. Its summit up there in the gloom seemed lighted; spots of blurred light were everywhere within it.

The whole scene of shadows seemed unreal. Like a dream. But as I saw those frantic figures scrambling within the threatened building, hacking futilely at its foundations to try and remove in time those dim, glowing bricks materializing from another realm—the stark, strange reality of it all was forced upon me.

We waited. How long I cannot say. Spectators of two realms, each to the other mere ghosts, standing there watching and waiting. For a time nothing happened throughout all the scene. And then a change was apparent in the crowds about the park. No longer were they watching us, the ghosts, but they were eyeing now the Woolworth Building. At first curiously, incredulous to believe the news which was spreading about. Then restlessly, and then, as orders evidently were passed to the troops and to the policemen, these began pushing and shoving at the people. The crowd resisted at first; moved reluctantly. Then a fear seemed to surge over them—fear growing to panic. They began trying to run—waves of them everywhere surging in panic away from the doomed building.

Hundreds went down underfoot, trampled upon in the streets by their fellows, mad, insane now with fear. And from every nearby building its occupants came tumbling out like frightened rats, scurrying out to join the panic of the streets. A chaos everywhere...

And we ghosts stood quiet and serene in its midst.

Brutar murmured. "Watch the great house. They know it is doomed. See, they have stopped their efforts in there— now at the last, trying to save themselves."

The Woolworth Building was emptying... Abandoned...

Breathlessly I stood and gazed upon the ghostly scene. The tremendous building towered there motionless. But presently I fancied it stirred; its graceful roof up there seemed swaying...shifting...or was it a trick of my straining vision? But then I saw it was not, for palpably the tower swayed— leaned. Then it leaned further—leaning until all at once I knew it could not recover. It poised, and then it was toppling.

A breathless instant. Slowly at first, like a felled forest giant, the great structure was coming down. Slowly, then with a rush it fell to the south—fell in great shattering segments. Crashed with a soundless crash upon the several blocks of nearby buildings. Crashed and tore with the thousands of tons of its weight, smothering everything beneath its crashing masonry and steel... A soundless chaotic scene of ruin and death over all those city blocks, with huge rising clouds of dirt and smoke mercifully to obscure it.

CHAPTER EIGHTEEN
The Rescuing Army

I STOOD gaping, every sense within me shuddering at that soundless scene of ruin and death. And then it came upon me that now I could escape. Brutar had turned triumphantly to his underlings. I heard his voice: "The first success! Now let us try the others!"

No one seemed noticing me. I turned and swept myself away into the darkness...

I was aware of the gray outlines of New York floating by above me...A dim idea was in my mind that I must rejoin Will and Thone...

Out there beneath the Westchester hills the silent mob of Brutar's ghostly followers still waited. Near them was the main body of his army, inactive, waiting here while he with his chosen few were experimenting upon New York!

Experimenting! This little experimental test, and it had brought down the Woolworth Building! What then would they do with a general attack?

I passed around the mob—silent, fleeing spectres—and sped again into darkness with no conscious thought of passing time or direction to my flight. Yet there must have been some instinct to guide me. The thought of Bee came strong. A growing triumph, a relief, told me I was nearing her; and I think now that it was her thought of me that guided my flight.

Darkness. But overhead lay the shadows of my own world. Winding gray hills; towns that lay like gray, colorless pictures in a book, queerly distorted a, I looked, upward and through them...

Shadows like myself were advancing from the gloom in front of me! A little group; behind them a vague sweep of shapes stretching out to seem a throng, a multitude. Thone! Will and Bee—with the rescuing army of the Big-City behind them!

The rescuing army...

THERE came upon me with that meeting a great surging knowledge of my love for Bee. My love, born up there in my own world. And then, in the realm of the Egos, stripped of the physical, a changed love that had faded to a vague affection—a knowledge that she was dear to me, but nothing more.

Now—in the Borderland once more, at least of half material substance, a very human love descended in a torrent. My arms went around her.

"Bee, my darling." And she responded to my caresses, kissing me with an eagerness, a longing undisguised. "Rob! I've been so frightened, not having you—" She murmured then that she loved me; and clung to me... The threshold of our own world.

But it was no time for lovemaking. I told Thone and Will what was transpiring, what already had come to pass, down there in New York. And with them we presently swept forward to the rescue.

Thone's army was at least as large as Brutar's; and it was not, like his, burdened by those who could not fight. In orderly array it advanced, and soon ahead of us we saw the shapes of Brutar's forces.

Strange ghostly battle into which now we plunged! I did not, could not fully understand it at the tine—but now I think I do. The very essence of it a physical inactivity. Fighting! The word to our Earthly minds is so full of movement! Yet a man battling with himself, pitting the good against the evil within himself, may sit in his easy chair and fight a fierce fight.

So it was here; unleashed forces of the mind, grappling silently—a struggle without rules of combat in which no quarter could be given, and which could only end by complete annihilation of one side or the other. I knew all this, and standing with Bee, Thone and Will on a dark eminence above the scene, I watched, breathlessly.

We were under that same little Westchester town. Its streets and houses lay shadowy above us. Ghostly people were up there—thronging the streets—gazing down with fear and awe at these flowing masses of ghosts advancing to battle.

The mob of Brutar's followers, frightened now, were huddled compactly. In area, they spread under perhaps half the village. And around them in a great concentric ring, Brutar's fighters massed. This movement Thone did not disturb.

"Let them," he said. "It's what I wish, to have them massed like that."

From our eminence—we were poised not very far beneath the ground level—we could see over the whole area of the battle, which was proceeding below us. The central mob who could not fight; the ring of Brutar's soldiers; and surrounding that, at a distance of some five hundred feet, another ring, Thone's fighters who now were massing to the attack.

"What will they do?" I murmured. But no one answered me, and soon I was answered by the scene itself. From both sides—Thone's army and Brutar's—little waves of the Thought-substance were flowing out over that segment between the opposing rings. Like slow-floating wisps of gray smoke from the heads of the fighters. Flowing across the space between the lines. Materializing steadily. Solidifying until I could almost imagine it might become a gray wall. But this was an illusion. It was merely thought—antagonistic, which would grip and hold like a net, no more.

The two opposing streams met in the center of that circular no-man's land between the lines. A chaos of blurred formless color was there. Not gray now. An angry red. The visible substances holding each other immovable. A boiling cauldron of red, with livid, lurid tongues like flame darting from it.

No sound. But I could feel it. A mental distress, as even at this distance its influence swept me. It was an uneasiness, a depression, a vague sense within me of a growing panic.

It seemed a deadlock. And then movement began—strategic movement. From one portion of his line Thone suddenly withdrew a number of his thinkers. They came sweeping around to our side. With this reinforcement we became stronger over here, and the red chaos surged inward. I saw it almost engulf the crouching Brutar fighters who were here opposing it. A few of them fell—ghostly shells lying inert—and above them a something luminous, the Ego-mind deranged, unhinged, hovering, then winging away into death.

A shape hurriedly approached us; a man with harried, anxious face. "Thone! We are too weak now upon the other side. The Red Death is almost upon us there! They want the thinkers back."

Thone ordered them back. He turned to me. "We will win, Rob."

But I could not see it so.

"Look!" He gestured. "There is a haze above the red. It passes inward—can't you see that? And they cannot stop it. They have not been trained, for they do not know what it is."

Above the red seething ring, where the opposing thoughts were meeting, I saw, as he had said, a haze. It seemed a dim purple. It was floating up and inward. Very tenuous, hardly to be noticed. An imponderable something.

Thone said, "A quality of our thought which they cannot combat since they do not know what it is—or realize perhaps its presence. But its influence will reach them in time."

He swung upon the attentive shapes near us. "Oh! Give orders not to hasten. Hold the deadlock. Keep them there. Do not hasten. We must drive up the others if we can. Brutar and the others—"

Brutar! His few picked men down there in New York working death and destruction! I had forgotten them completely. Thone issued other orders. "If thoughts of distress come from here—let the thoughts out. They may reach Brutar—bring him back to help his battle here. Let out their thoughts that way." He gestured toward New York. "And if we drive Brutar and his men up here, let them in."

Other orders. A hundred or two of our fighters withdrew from the line. One here and there; ceasing to fight, coming toward Thone, forming behind us. A picked force with which we were to descend into New York.

And soon, leaving the scene here, we sped under the gray shadows of Westchester, southward toward the city. And in time, came upon it. New York. Splendid giant. Like some great helpless lion standing harried. Cuffed, wounded, stricken. Unable to fight back. Amazed, bewildered, yet undaunted, ready to fight.

But helpless.

CHAPTER NINETEEN
The Stricken City

THE little glowing bricks had been spread in scores of places. The acres of tumbled masonry that once reared aloft in proud splendor—the Woolworth Building—lay still smoking. Other buildings were down. Lower Manhattan—its pile of monuments to the engineering skill of man—was interspersed with areas of ruin. A smoke pall hung over everything. Through it as we arrived I saw another giant building come down...

A warship lay in the upper harbor. Small boats were clustered around it. Over its decks and within its structure, men were frantically rushing. It stood there, a shadow on the shadowy water, the embodiment of impregnable power; the small anxious boats around it like milling pygmies trying futilely to help its distress.

Then men began pouring from it. The little boats took them and made off. Alone it lay there. Motionless. Then there came a surge of its giant bulk upward—a torrent waterspout as of a great mine exploding beside it. Bow down, it began to sink.

The Statue of Liberty fell—head down, with torch plunging like a falling symbol...

The great Fort Wadsworth guarding the Narrows, as though an earthquake had torn it apart, rose and shook and fell into a shapeless mass. A small police boat was scurrying by in a panic. The tumbling white waves engulfed it...

The Brooklyn Bridge lay broken and fallen. Its dangling cables hung like rent cobwebs ripped apart by a giant, ruthless hand. Figures of men were clinging to parts of it.

Death and destruction was everywhere. But there were soldiers grimly standing in Battery Park, machine-guns idly standing. Another warship, unattacked, belching belligerent smoke, moving majestically around the Battery from one river to another.

A harried lion. Undaunted. But helpless to fight.

BENEATH the shadows of the lower Hudson we came upon Brutar and his clustered cohorts. The devastation was slackening; the bricks had done their work. Brutar was doubtless thinking of rejoining his people up there under the little Westchester town. He saw our shapes, and started north. We followed. Urging him on, but not attacking.

Thone began, "Once we get them all together up there—all of them together—" But he did not finish.

Our lines let them through. It was a crescent battle line now, open to the south. But when Brutar swept in we closed it as before.

The scene here had changed somewhat since we left it. The lurid red of the opposing thought-streams still held balanced between the lines of the fighters. But in one place it was indented now far into Brutar's territory—a red gash like a wound gaping amid his huddled throng. And I noticed, too, that the dim purple haze hung now like an aura close above the heads of our enemies.

I asked Thone about it. He said, "Those who are not fighters in there are beginning to feel our thoughts. Perhaps even they begin to suspect what awaits them. Soon the fighters also will know."

He spoke quietly, but on a note of calm certainty that in the end we would triumph. From that same height we watched the scene. Almost immovable, struggling ghosts—gray translucent shapes to my vision as now I regarded them. Yet—I wondered—were not those shapes of Brutar's people more solid than our own? A vague shudder mingled with triumph unholy, swept over me. Was it fancy, or was there indeed a change?

I could see Brutar, or at least a shape I assumed to be his, raised upon a height in the center of his forces; his arms waving; his soundless voice doubtless exhorting his fighters to greater effort. The fog of purple haze swirled about him, tinting, but not obscuring, for it seemed utterly transparent. Was it my fancy that Brutar's shape was of changing aspect?

And then I was aware of an uneasiness growing in the mob huddled there in the midst of the fighting. A stirring. A ripple of movement. Spreading like the ripples of a pebble thrown into a pond; spreading until abruptly the mob was surging, struggling to break the bonds of its own protecting ring of fighter's.

The fighters felt the press of the throng behind them. Their efforts wavered. With diverted minds their thought-stream weakened. At once the red tumult moved in upon them.

But Thone called his orders and a score of shapes relayed them throughout our circular investing ring. I could not understand it. We were not to press our advantage. Our fighters lessened visibly the strength of their attack. And our antagonists in a moment recovered.

Thone said quietly, "No, Rob—if we were to force in there now and overwhelm them, there would be many minds unhinged, but not driven irrevocably away. They might return. It is my aim to destroy them completely—mind and body—annihilation!"

Savage purpose, savagely expressed! But he added, "It is best—and I think, more merciful."

CHAPTER TWENTY
The Destruction of the Ghosts

THERE came presently a sudden change to this silent battle. For the purely mental, abruptly was substituted a semblance of physical struggle. The two mingled. In the Ego-world it would not have been possible; but here in the Borderland, these bodies of half-material substance abruptly found themselves capable of it. From physical immobility there sprang movement; a panic at first, but Brutar quelled it and organized it into a concerted rush. His mob, his fighters, began pressing forward in a single direction. The Borderland slope lay well beneath the ground level of the village overhead; but off to the left there seemed an area in the outskirts of the town where the slope and the ground of Earth reached a common level. And Brutar's people were pressing that way.

They surged forward then were forced back—surging and rebounding as one would press against a yielding but entangling net. Our lines, and theirs, and the red tumult of conflict surged with them; bending, but the whole scene holding its contour. And I saw that very slowly, with each forward sweep and rebound they were gaining in their direction.

I heard Thone beside me addressing Will. "They will never make it. They will be too late." He seemed to realize something. "Those people up there in the town, Will—they must escape! Abandon the town! All of them escape—now before it's too late!"

Will said, "If we could only communicate with them. Do you suppose we could?" And Bee eagerly put in, "Let's try. Let Rob and me try. We will go up there to the level."

They explained it all to me then. Horrible, sinister, shuddering outcome! Gruesome! Of course, the Earth-people in the town must escape...

Bee and I together took ourselves up the Borderland slope to the outskirts of the village where the slope was level with the ground. We were now half a mile beyond this spectral town, which was thronged with ghostly vehicles and ghostly people staring in wonderment down at the battle scene.

WE came to the common level, stood upon a spectral road with a few wraiths of houses lining it. There seemed no people here—they were all crowding the town to gaze at the struggling ghosts directly beneath them there.

"No one is around here, Bee." But no sooner had I said it than we saw, standing by a fence nearby, a ghost warily regarding us. A man in uniform, a State trooper I thought. He appeared, standing there alone, to have no desire to approach us. But I waved. And Bee waved. We carefully advanced upon him—carefully, for fear of startling him into flight. Gesturing, smiling with every effort to appear friendly. He understood us at last; came to the middle of the road, and there we joined him.

Fantastic meeting! Ghosts, all of us, standing there in a group, gesturing. I put out my hand as a friend, and his came to meet it. Touched it? Had a billion million miles of Space and Eons of Time been between us we could hardly have been further apart!

But at last we made him understand. An ingenious fellow! He took a shadowy paper and pencil from his pocket and wrote what he thought we intended to convey to him; and we read it and nodded and smiled—grimly, for this was grim business indeed—grim, horrible!

When at last he knew, astonishment, terror was upon him. And he was off down the road at a run, waving his arms, shouting no doubt, screaming to everyone his terrible warning...

We rejoined Thone upon the height overlooking the struggle. He murmured, "I see you were successful. And just in time—this is almost over now."

The battle lines still held. But what a change was come to our enemies! There was no mistaking it now—their bodies were materializing. The purple haze carrying the malignant influence of our fighters was forcing their bodies into the Earth-state!

The town above us, warned by our messenger was emptying. Vehicles—shadowy moving shapes of cars and wagons—were scurrying out of it over all the roads. The houses were empty; the roads all thronged with fugitives on foot. Empty-handed; and families trudging with what little worldly goods they could carry in their arms. Wagons and cars piled high with household furnishings hastily rescued. The lines of pedestrians urged, lashed to greater haste by frightened officials. An exodus from death into safety...

The end came suddenly, unexpectedly swiftly. Thousands of ghostly bodies, there beneath the ground of the village abruptly leaping over the last gap into material being. *In the ground*—the earth, the rock—the very atoms of these foreign bodies intermingled, blended to their essence with the atoms of the rock and soil. And suddenly leaping into solidity...

The scene everywhere seemed to shudder. Its gray details slurred into a blur, a formless chaos of power unleashed, a soundless rumble, a sweep of tumbling movement. Upward, with a burst—an infinity of newly created entities demanding space. Space! Demanding it; heaving upward over the path of least resistance to find it...

As though in the bowels of the earth a pent-up volcano had suddenly broken forth, the abandoned village heaved into the air—rose, shattered apart, and fell in a tumbled waste. An earthquake, a very cataclysm of nature outraged...

A shattered, tumbled mass of wreckage where a moment before there had been a village... Fire leaped to the last destruction... Smoke rolled up in great spiraling clouds...

And visible down beneath the ruin, a ring of victorious shimmering ghosts, standing awed and alone in the empty darkness...

CHAPTER TWENTY-ONE
Each to His Own Allotted Portion

WE STOOD in the Borderland with Thone and Ala.

"You will not return to our Ego-world?" said Thone. It was a statement in tone, rather than a question. "You are right, friends. Each to his own, as the Creator intended. Your world, better for you—but ours, best of them all, for us."

Ala was standing close by Will. So near was she to our Earth-state, here in the Borderland, that I knew she had felt for Will those stirrings we call love. And now she was fighting them.

He touched her. "Could you not find it best to come with my sister and me, Ala?"

But she shook her head. "No. Father speaks truth. One should hold in contentment his allotted portion." But I think it tore at her with a new, very human temptation. "Goodbye," she said resolutely.

It wrenched at us all. Friendship, even over so brief an interval, cannot be lightly broken. We told ourselves we would not break it. Some day, some time, we would again come together.

"Goodbye." Soundlessly it echoed within us. Will, Bee and I stood silent as we watched them trudge away into the shadows and the darkness.

Each to his own allotted portion.

Thone had assured us that our natural tendency of body would be to resume an Earth-existence from this adjacent Borderland. And Will had formerly returned and found it easier than staying. We located, after roaming a time, that corner of Will's own garden where the ground level of Earth coincided with the Borderland slope...

Solidity! Again—at last—we were solid, human-wraiths no longer. Will had gone on into the house; Bee and I lingered in the garden. Blessed sounds and sights and odors. We could hear the murmur of insect life; hear the night breeze stirring the leaves, feel it fanning our hot cheeks. The roses and honeysuckle were heavily, thrillingly odorous. The moon bathed us with its pale silver fire.

I took Bee in my arms. She came, willingly, eagerly, trembling with this newfound world of love. And returned my kisses, and clung to me.

"Each to his own, Bee darling. How good this world of ours seems! I never appreciated it before. Did you?"

"No! No, never!"

But I appreciated it now.

THE END